DAVID PLANTE • ESSENTIAL STORIES

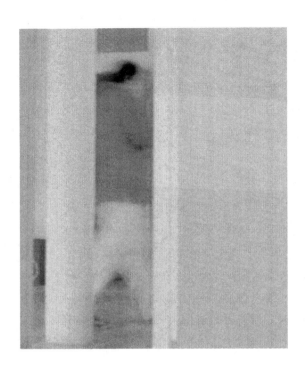

David Plante

Essential Stories

Grey Suit Editions

First published in 2022 by
Grey Suit Editions, an affiliate
of Phoenix Publishing House Ltd

British Library Cataloguing in Publication Data
A C.I.P. catalogue record for this book is available
from the British Library

ISBN 978-1-903006-27-6

Designed and typeset in Monotype Bembo by Anvil
Photograph by Ellen Phelon
Printed and bound in the United Kingdom
by Hobbs the Printers Ltd

Grey Suit Editions
33 Holcombe Road, London N17 9AS
https://greysuiteditions.co.uk/

Contents

The History of Love 8

A Movement in the Soul 12

The Sea 16

Mother 18

Abstract Thought 21

War 23

Diary 25

Gravity and Grace 26

A Prayer 28

Birth 31

Pornography 32

Prayer 36

The Beautiful Young Man 40

Rock and Sunlight 57

Reconciliation 60

Reason 63

The Setting Sun 66

The Two Selves 70

The Smell of Honeysuckle 72

Singing the Universal World 74

Sleep 77

Weather 80

Strange Signals 82

The Fall 84

The Metaphor 94

The Canoe 95

Appeal 98

Civilization 101

Order and Disorder 104

Proof of the Existence of the Mother of God 107

Purification 110

The Vision 114

A Mother and a Son 126

The Wind 139

Grief 146

The Silver Conch Shell 158

Our Lady of the Beautiful Window 160

*Essential
Stories*

The History of Love

Start with: amo, amas, amat, amemus, amatis, amant.

As he spoke, holding up what he called a jar as if in salutation, I noted a scar on his jaw. We were in the midst of standing men, mostly aged, some old, and some young men, all holding what he called jars, all of us in dim light. I was holding an empty jar. He asked me if I would like a refill, and smiled, a spirited smile, when I thanked him. He pressed his way among the men, aged men talking with other aged men, or a few aged men talking to young men, but mostly aged men alone, looking about. He came back, his smile more spirited, confident, with two refills. He handed the jar to me so I must reach with my left hand, and he, his jar in his left hand, held out his right hand for me to shake. I did. His smile now a light laugh, a light laugh of confidence, perhaps a light laugh of relief, he told me his name.

I never did ask him about the scar.

I invited him home.

He was thirty five and I sixty five.

In my bed, to hold him, naked, was for me to be thirty five, to be thirty five and to have a tight scalp of short soft hair, to have a brow, cheek bones, nose, lips,

9

jaw, neck, clavicle clearly and beautifully defined was to have a long, lean body, smoothly curving at the shoulders, the thighs, the buttocks, oh, and all the more clearly and beautifully defined in the almost dark of the room, his scar gone.

He pulled back, perhaps suddenly seeing me as I was, which made me see myself as I was. His eyes shone.

Empedocles the pre-Socratic philosopher wrote:

That all be reunited into one by an act of Love.

Our love-making was simple.

He spent the night, cuddled to me.

We slept together until late in the morning.

In the wan light, he looked wan, and said little.

At our late breakfast, both bathed and he in clean underclothes I gave him, he told me he didn't have enough money to return to where he lived.

Trying to joke, I asked him what he would have done if I had not taken him home? His smile was crooked.

He did not look well. He did not look well.

In his pale face, the scar appeared recent, red.

He spoke well, and I was more attentive to the individual words than his general topic, wondering how, through him, this still young man, should be articulated such ancient words as: I, you, us.

He stopped talking.

I said, You're not well.

I'm not.

What do you want that I can give you?

He lowered his head and said, I want to believe in life after death.

And I said, There is.

He looked up at me, not smiling.

I gave him money and made him swear he would contact me when he was back to wherever he lived.

Goodbye, he said, and, love.

I was away for months, in another city, in another country. Returned, I heard that he had died.

Make this the center of all writing: a prayer to the dead, a prayer to the dead, a prayer in thanksgiving for all the words the dead have left us:

I love, you love, he/she loves, we love, you love, they love.

A Movement in the Soul

On a walk in the town, my daughter and I were passing a brick, medieval church, the doors open, and she went inside. I followed, hesitant, because I wasn't sure we were allowed to enter, or if, more likely, I didn't want to enter. But my strong-minded daughter thought that there was no reason why she shouldn't be allowed to enter anywhere.

The vast interior appeared to be filled with a dark, cold mist, in the far distance a few votive candles burning, but nothing else, and she went into that mist, and, again, I followed her to where the candles were burning in a stand before a side altar.

Above the altar was a polychrome wooden statue of a slim young woman wearing a long pink dress cinched in tightly just below her small breasts and falling in rigid folds to the tips of her pointed shoes. Her hair was yellow and braided about her head, her neck was slender and long, and her delicate face, the paint finely cracked, was pink. She held out her hands, large hands with long fingers, as if in surprise, though her face was calm. She was where she had been for centuries.

I turned and walked away to leave the church, and when I turned back to see if my daughter was behind me I saw that she was kneeling on the first step of the altar and looking up at the statue in the dim candlelight. I went out into the square and waited for her; my shoulders hunched against the damp cold.

I had very little to say to my daughter, not even in a café where we sat at a table in the corner and I ordered cups of coffee corrected, as is said, with rum, and after the coffee we continued to sit and watched people at the long marble bar drink their small, thick cups of coffee and go, while we, having nothing better to do, lingered.

At the back of the café was a white grand piano.

My daughter asked me, What do you think it means, saying, 'How moved I am'?

I answered, I suppose some movement is meant.

What movement?

I told myself to pay attention and said, When you feel a movement in yourself that's greater than you ever thought you could feel.

You've felt that?

I have.

When was that? she asked.

I wanted to say, When you were born. I wanted to let her know she moved me, that my love for her moved me. But she would have sensed that I was lying, that at her birth I turned against her and her mother, that I had never loved her, that my lack of love inspired in me despair. That was the movement in me.

What is the truest thing said? Pythagoras asked, and answered, That men are evil.

I didn't answer her question, because the answer would have given her reason enough to think I had had every reason to have been in prison.

My daughter announced, It's dogma, that to be a real believer you have to believe that the holy mother is a virgin.

Where did you learn that?

I learned it.

And you believe in that?

I believe.

You honestly do? I asked.

Yes, I do.

Someone sat at the white grand piano and played the music of an opera aria.

My daughter said, All you have to do to believe in something is to be moved by it, that's all.

But it can't be, that a mother can be a virgin.

No, it can't be. But you can be moved by something that can't be'.

I felt myself draw far back from her to see her as if from a far distance, her voice, too, coming from a far distance.

And she laughed, and I thought, she wasn't serious.

I asked, How is your mother?

She asked me to say hello.

And hello to her.

We listened to the man playing the piano, who began to sing the aria.

My daughter led the way as we walked the worn stone paved medieval streets of the town. Snow began to fall. My daughter – my beautiful, intelligent daughter – was withdrawn in her thinking, then she said, as if she had not ever before occurred to her to consider what came to her now with wonder, Think about it, just think about is, belief in a virgin mother. She laughed. A virgin mother.

And she held out her hands to the falling snow.

The Sea

We met on a ferry that transported lorries and cars in its vast holds, and passengers on the upper decks. We shared a cabin.

I'd hoped to be alone in the cabin, as there were not many passengers, and no doubt he'd hoped too, for as he unpacked his bag on his narrow berth he said, as if to himself, that the crew always put passengers together to save themselves from doing up rooms used singly. I thought I should respond, as we were, after all, to share the same space to sleep in, and I said, laughing lightly, I don't snore. He looked at me and said he was sorry, he did, but only when he was lying on his back, so I must shake him and he would turn over and, over, he didn't snore.

I don't have to comment on the strangeness of sleeping in the same space with someone you don't know.

We were both about the same age, fifty, and bore the effects of our fifty years with thinning hair, nasal hair, and dull teeth.

I asked him to join me in the lounge for a drink.

Again I don't have to comment on how people who are strangers to one another reveal themselves.

He was in a great agitation. He didn't explain the circumstances that had caused the agitation. It seemed to me that the particulars didn't interest him, that he was in an expansive state that was overwhelming to him and beyond any particulars. He spoke about that state as if it possessed him and in talking to me he might, a little, dispossess himself of it.

I can't any longer, he said, I can't, I can't bear it.

I, perhaps not all that interested, didn't try to learn what it was.

He closed his eyes and became silent and rested his head against the back of his chair, and I saw from the expressions twitching the muscles of his face that many different thoughts were causing the twitching. Then one thought seemed to make him raise his head and open his eyes and look at me.

He laughed a hearty laughed and said, Roll on, roll on, deep, dark sea.

Mother

I, her mother, advised her to have the baby, to be born out of wedlock, as the old-fashioned expression then had it.

Supposing the baby is destined to be, oh, at least happy in the world, how can you deprive anyone of happiness in the world? But supposing the baby is destined to more than happiness, is destined to be someone of influence in the world – someone who will make a difference to the world for the better, a great politician, a great scientist, a great poet? I know how much you believe that the world is evil and that no one should be born into it, but you know how much I think your belief is naïve.

She said to me, And your belief in a world that can be made good, that isn't naïve?

Yes, yes. But I feel so deeply that you can bring up a baby, on your own, to disprove everything you believe about the world. You can do that, I know you can do that, and doing that will make you realize the world is a good place, a place for happiness and goodness. Have the baby, my dear, dear daughter, and prove to yourself that there is happiness and goodness in the world. Give yourself and the baby a chance. Dear, dear, darling daughter, give the baby a chance at least to be happy.

I never told her that I, myself unmarried at the time, had considered terminating the pregnancy that was fulfilled in her, my beautiful, unhappy daughter.

She said, The father would want to have nothing to do with the baby.

You're free, then, to bring up your darling as you wish, to inspire him or her with, oh, your faith.

She frowned. Faith?

I must be careful, as she had severely rejected, hardly into her teens, any belief in God, and I, she knew, retained a non-denominational belief in God. That I even suggest she have the baby because God so willed would have had her make an appointment immediately with a clinic. She was nineteen.

Belief that the world can be made better.

Her face became calm and she looked away, into the woods that surrounded us, woods in which deer sometimes appeared in sunlight and disappeared in shadow.

That the world be made a just, righteous, a loving world.

The baby was born deformed in its small body.

My daughter, who was severe, would not accept an apology from me, and I gave none. Nor would she live with me, though I offered her all my support. But I often went to her house, which was a short walk along a path through the woods. I went often, and found her — what can I say? — dutiful, but not loving, no, not loving. And though my daughter would never reproach me, the way she looked at me when I entered unexpectedly made me feel she had ceased loving me, if she ever had loved me.

Watching her bathe the baby, whose spine was so deformed he would never be able to stand, I dared myself to say, as unemotionally as possible, You will have to inspire in him more love than in any other child.

The baby appeared to take deep pleasure in the warm bath, and, splashing, laughed while his mother held his naked body.

I said, He will be happy, and I turned away.

My daughter did not reproach me, but, yes, I reproached myself, and, I tell you truthfully (I wish it had been otherwise), I reproached myself all the more when one late afternoon, when the trees of the woods were slowly and solemnly dropping their leaves, I entered my daughter's house and, going from room to room, found her and her baby boy, three months old, on the large four-poster bed in her bedroom, she dandling him so his crooked body was suspended in the air, his bare feet as if dancing, and he was laughing, and my daughter too was laughing, she so suddenly loving that I was startled. Without her noticing me, I withdrew down the passage and out of the house. And my reproach to myself, which now shocked me for my recognizing the cause, was that I had made a mistake, that they would forever be isolated, my darling daughter and her darling son, in their love for each other, which would have nothing to do with the world.

Abstract Thought

She said, I don't at all understand abstract thought, not at all. What is meant by the eternal?

That's like asking me what my stories are about, he said, which question I can never answer.

You can't say what your stories are about?

I can't.

They sat on a bench near the church and together looked down at the sea, and were silent.

To him, there was peace in the monotonous sound of the sea waves indifferent to the long ago past when there was no one to hear, indifferent to the present, indifferent to the future when there would be no one to hear.

He reached for her hand and smiled at her with the wonder of this young woman in the dawn light sitting by him, and she smiled and drew back her hand to hold his arm.

How could he tell her what the eternal was? How could he tell her that he believed their love for each other was eternal? How could he tell her that there was salvation in the indifferent eternal, indifferent to him, to her, to them together, and in that indifference was eternity, whose meaning was so vast there was no knowing what the meaning could be? How could he make that believable to her, how could he make that believable in a story? Stories, he thought, were indifferent to what they were about; they could be about nothing, or could be about what was so vast he himself was never able to say, so vast their meaning was their own, not his, because eternity had its own meaning, not his, and, yes, he believed that there was salvation in eternity.

The ferry was coming, its lights lit; he thought they would soon go to the landing place and board to return to the mainland and their hotel room and then their separate lives, but they remained a while longer.

A little sob rose in his throat. She heard it and she held his arm close to her.

No, he did not know what his stories were about.

Time for us to return, she said.

In their hotel room, he watched her on the bed asleep while he ate a slice of melon, and he thought, if he were to write a story about their love he would put in, incidentally, the slice of melon.

War

He lay in bed in the ward and he wondered why there were hospitals set up for the wounded and the dying, if the object of war was to wound and kill. It wasn't enough to think that the soldiers on the side he had fought for had to be saved, because, finally, no one was saved, not on the side he fought for and not on the side of the soldiers who fought against his side. They were all meant to be wounded, all meant to be killed, and there would be no winning, but only losing. So why not accept that everyone lost, and let the wounded lie where they had been wounded, let the dying die?

He couldn't stand the question, Why war? He couldn't stand it because it was a banal question, and the answer to the question would be banal. Even to say there was no understanding was banal, and better not try to understand.

His mind was one with his body in pain.

Understand what? he asked himself, understand what?

He prayed for his body to be released from the pain, there in bed among many beds of men moaning in pain; he prayed, oh, not to understand why such pain, a banal understanding of a banal question, but for pain to be itself understanding, understanding released from his pain to become all pain, greater than his, greater than all the pain together of the men screaming from their beds.

It was happening, it was, the slow coming together of his body straining for release in pain.

Let it happen, he prayed, let it happen.

Diary

He was left his lover's diaries, all in Greek, which he could not read, not without studying every word and as often as not having to look up the word in a bi-lingual dictionary. He was determined, however, to read the passages in the diaries that his lover had underlined. He imagined himself to be someone searching for faith, intent on finding out in texts arcane to him proof of his faith, which required concentrated study, and, more, rigorous discipline in centring all his life on the proof. He read

ΟΡΕΑΣ ΕΦΟΒΟΣ

which words he did not understand at first reading, but which suddenly revealed themselves as

BEAUTIFUL BOY

and, aroused with suspicion of his lover's faithfulness, he became obsessed with reading his lost lover's diaries to find out who this beautiful boy was, about whom his lover had said nothing.

But there was nothing more than that:

ΟΡΕΑΣ ΕΦΟΒΟΣ

Gravity and Grace

I, a professor, asked my students, What do you believe is common to all humans, to every single individual one of us?

We were in a room where the light was between day and dusk, not dim enough to switch on lamps but still vaguely clear enough for the faces of my students, sitting around a large rectangular table, to be those of individuals.

They were silent.

Isn't there anything you can think of that transcends the individual world to the universal?

My students, I have to say, came from many different worlds, so different from one another that I sometimes thought the only universal among us, including myself, was our more or less common language, English.

Come on, I prompted, come on, one of you speak.

And a young man with a close-cut black beard that defined his jaw and chin sharply, said, Gravity.

Oh? I asked. Why, gravity?

We all, wherever we come from, have the experience of falling, of knowing that if we throw ourselves off from a high place we won't rise, but fall.

That can be interpreted in many different ways, I said.

Yes, but the common experience is falling because of some force that pulls us down, doesn't lift us up so we rise.

He was a bright student, and he inspired me.

After the class, I returned to my home, where my wife was feeding our infant child, in a high-chair; our baby boy kept dropping his spoon over the side of the high-chair, over and over, and my wife each time picked the spoon up and rinsed it and gave the spoon back to our baby, who ate a little then, smiling, dropped the spoon again.

I can't stop him, she said.

I said, He's learning about gravity.

And I thought, there is grace in learning about gravity, there is grace in the universality of gravity, which has entirely to do with the rough round earth we live on, all of us, all, together.

We fall, I thought, we fall, let us know, all the world, that we fall.

A Prayer

We walked together below the ruins, once the ramparts of a walled-in city.

He said to me, No, I can't believe in God, I can't. Over the centuries, an untold, a truly untold number of prayers have been said to God for God's help, and I can't understand why God hasn't answered every single one if God is a loving God. If God has answered some, they're very few compared to those untold number of prayers that were not answered, prayers cried out by the desperate for God's help, whole walled-in cities crying out for God to deliver them from massacre. And I won't accept that God is testing our faith. The test is unreasonable, and if there is a God, God is supposed to be a reasonable as well as a loving God. No, no.

I asked him, Did you once believe?

And he answered, I once believed.

And you stopped believing.

I more than said a prayer, I implored in prayer for God's help, and God didn't help. He laughed. I needed God's help as a matter of life and death.

Yours?

Someone else's life or death.

And this someone else died.

Died.

I said, The streets of this city once ran with blood, rivulets of blood along the gutters.

He was insistent: And God did not help, not answering even one prayer by one old woman hiding in a doorway to be saved.

He stopped to study the old worn stone paving.

I'm very tired, he said.

You're in mourning.

Yes, mourning.

I'm sorry.

If only God had saved him, he said. If only God had shown proof — what I would have taken as proof — of God's existence by answering my fervent prayer. I so wanted him to live. I so needed him to live. I felt the world, the whole world, needed him to live for proof of God's existence for the world. I would have let the world know, God exists, God answered my prayer, I would have gone around the world, gone around with him, alive, to every city, to let everyone know that I had proof, that God saved my loved one, there beside me. He asked, Do I sound crazy?

I wondered if he was, but I answered, No.

The vast, vast number, the untold number of those who, over centuries and centuries, of all religions, all, pleaded in prayer for God to help, and God didn't. And I'm among them now, I'm one with them.

I thought: I can't help him.

Thank you, he said, thank you for listening to me. Thank you.

I didn't leave.

He said, You see, he believed in prayer. Up until the end, he prayed. He prayed and prayed. You should have seen him in the end, as thin as a saint in the highest state of grace, shining, yes, shining right through his bones and skin, and smiling as he prayed. And up until the end I thought that the miracle might happen, that his prayer would be answered and he would be restored to the full-bodied beauty he was, my love, my love, restored to his great beauty, my love, restored to in his great beauty back into my arms, and I, I would love him all the more, my love, because I would believe that God saved him, that he was proof that there was a God.

I reached out a hand to shake his before leaving him.

He said, And now I want to tell everyone, tell the whole world, that there is no God.

Birth

Mother and daughter, they were sitting together on a glider under a grape arbour on the grounds of the asylum, the grapes hanging in ripe bunches, so ripe bees hummed among them. The daughter thought that her mother and she, rocking slowly back and forth, must be together for a reconciliation that she had for years wanted and her mother now wanted because she was dying.

And there seemed to be, in the loose way her mother sat back among the cushions of the glider, an acceptance of everything she had once refused to accept, an acceptance even of her death. Her voice was as soft as the evening air.

She said, Listen –

Her daughter did listen, and heard, perhaps, the fluttering hum of the bees.

I want to tell you, her mother said, then stopped and again the silence seemed to flutter with the hum of the bees.

Pornography

At the house of a friend whose parents were away, he for the first time watched a pornographic film, and he was shocked that he had never himself fantasized about the various sexual positions enacted by the man and the woman. His remaining and overwhelming sense was that there must be more to sex than what he'd seen on the screen.

This sense was elaborated in him in his early maturity, when, undressing a girl he had not yet seen naked, he wondered if there might be a surprise to him in her very body that would make the sex with her different from sex with any other girl, and sex would be wonderful.

He was not a bad person, but he admitted he was, whenever a sexual urge came to him, a fantasist. And he admitted that he was always disappointed in his fantasy, though he made sure the girl never thought he was disappointed in her, but was loving.

In love, he married, and his love was constant.

He was with his wife in a hotel room by the sea, on an off season holiday. He was now in his middle years, and had no children, though he wanted a child, or had wanted a child, as had his wife. He went to the open windows onto a terrace to look out at the beach and the sea. His wife came to look with him.

He said, I think I'll go for a walk along the beach.

Alone? his wife asked.

Do you mind?

She smiled the smile she always gave him of her understanding when he wished to be alone.

He loved his wife, of course he loved his wife, and would always love her; and she knew that since they had married he had not been unfaithful to her, nor would he ever be.

He kept reminding himself: sex is the same, really, with every woman, so why should he imagine sex would be different with any other woman?

The beach, misted, was almost empty.

This happened: as he walked along he saw a woman where the surf broke on the shore, broke in long waves that ebbed more violently than they flowed, and the woman was screaming. As he went to her, she shouted, My daughter, my daughter is caught in the undertow! In the mist, he could just make out a head swept forward then swept back more. He kicked off his sandals, ripped off his shirt and shorts, and dived into the waves and swam against the undertow, always more and more separated from the girl flailing in the rising and falling water. When he reached her she was submerged, and when he brought her, face up, to the surface, he saw that she was dead.

Her mother was up to her knees in the surf, her arms out, perhaps hopeful. Able now to stand in the surf, he brought the little girl's body to the shore, lay her chest down on the sand and pressed again and again on her back, clumsily, as he wasn't sure he was doing what was right. Over them stood the girl's mother, stunned still until, with a wild gesture, she pushed him away from her daughter's body and picked up her daughter in her arms, the child's head resting on an arm, water draining from her open mouth, her legs hanging over her mother's other arm.

Her mother screamed at him, Go away, go away, go away! as if he was responsible for the death of her daughter.

He knew he must not go away, but went to a distance and, wet and shivering in spasms, sat on the sand.

Finally, with whatever was required of him to state to the police, he walked slowly back to the hotel, and on the way stopped often, still shaking in spasms, and a sense of terrible loss came over him – more than the loss of the girl he hadn't known, more than the loss if the girl had been his daughter, loss of more than he could imagine.

His wife was coming towards him as he was standing still, and all he did was look at her for her to put her arms about him to hold him.

He said, I tried to save a drowning girl, but failed.

She held him more tightly, as to support him to their

hotel room, where she drew a bath, sat on the edge of the tub, and even dried him when he rose.

Naked, he held her and rested his head on her shoulder. The spasms gave way to yawns, yawns that shook him and left him feeling weak. And yet, pressed against her body, he felt an erection rising into her skirt. He pressed his forehead against her cheek, then drew his cheek against her cheek and kissed her.

He asked, Will you come to bed with me?

Hurriedly, she pulled the counterpane from the bed, and folded back the blankets and sheet.

Prayer

He visited his mother in the nursing home. She was sitting alone by her bed, and she didn't have her false teeth in, so her mouth appeared puckered within wrinkles, and her nose large. She was looking at the floor.

He said, Ma, and she raised her head to look towards him, but not at him, and he wondered if her sight was going.

Ma, he repeated, it's me.

Oh yes, she said, it's you.

He leaned over her and kissed her cheek, and she said, They've lost my false teeth.

Who did?

She made a gesture that included anyone. They get the false teeth mixed up, so I tried some that didn't fit me. Maybe someone tried mine on and they fit, and they were kept. I don't know. Maybe someone died with my false teeth, and was buried with them.

Sitting on the edge of her bed, he said, I'll find out for you.

She smiled and revealed wet gums. It don't matter.

He corrected her. It doesn't matter.

Right, it doesn't matter. She spoke carefully. You have always corrected my grammar.

But it does matter.

Why?

Well, I think that having your teeth is like speaking grammatically, it makes a good impression.

I suppose.

I'll go ask about your teeth.

Not now.

All right, he said and asked, Have you been treated well?

Well, yes, well enough.

He repeated what he had repeated every time he visited her. You know I would have you home if only I were able to give you the special treatment you require.

I know, I know.

And he repeated, to reassure her. You're my mother, after all.

She laughed a small laugh. And you're my son. Funny, how that seems funny to me now.

Funny in what way?

Oh, I gave birth to you, that's sure, and I brought you up alone after your father left, at least until you went off to boarding school, but I don't feel I have been a real mother to you.

This shocked him. What would you have done if you'd been a real mother to me?

Oh, I would have taught you something you really needed, something that would have made you happy.

I'm not unhappy.

Aren't you?

I try not to be.

I'm sorry I wasn't the mother I wish I'd been.

Please don't say that.

Well, I sit here hour after hour, and I think about the past. I wish I could choose what to remember, but so many remembrances from the past come to me on their own, and I can't stop them. And I remember seeing you off to boarding school and thinking, I should keep him home with me, I should be a real mother to him. You see, she said quietly, I feel I sinned as a mother.

Oh, Ma, please, please don't say that.

But it's what I feel.

He was earnest. Then I forgive you, though I can't see that there's anything to forgive you for, not anything you did or didn't do as my mother.

She said, I pray to the Holy Mother to forgive me.

He put his hand to his forehead. Please, Ma, he said, please.

Anyway, she said, I pray, I do pray to the Holy Mother to forgive all the sins that are committed in the world.

That would take a lot of forgiveness.

A lot, I know, but she is the Mother us all.

He shook his head a little. He suddenly thought that his mother would die soon, but what the feeling was that was roused in him at the thought he didn't know, perhaps some longing.

On the bus back to his apartment, he thought of his mother sitting alone by her bed, thought of how much she, a widow, had done for him. From her pay, he had been at boarding school, and on his visits home he had taught her grammar, and that was all he had done for her, his mother. He had not been a good son.

Rain was falling when he descended from the bus, and he felt rainwater drip through his hair, but, wet as he was, he didn't want to return to where he lived. He had no idea why.

So much was occurring to him that left him wondering why it all did, why feelings came to him without his knowing why and without his being able to name the feelings. He stood in the entrance to a closed shop and watched the rain fall.

Holy Mother, he thought, Holy Mother of God.

The Beautiful Young Man

When I went to the porter's lodge with my suitcase, I was politely given the key to my rooms. In the evening, wandering along passageways, I came to a room where fellows were gathered, or I presumed, because of their academic gowns, that they were fellows. Some fellows were sitting alone, some were gathered in small groups, and I approached one of these and introduced myself.

He was a Divine of the Church who had written books on the Eucharist.

He asked me, Where is your gown? You must wear a gown, or we won't know who you are.

I don't have a gown, I said.

You have dining rights at high table, don't you?

I said, I think I do.

Then you're entitled to, and should, wear a gown.

When he took me to the butler in the pantry to explain that I would be eating in, if that were possible. Very well, the butler said, but he wasn't so forthcoming about the gown. He said, looking towards the ceiling, Well, sir, I'm not sure the writer in residence is entitled to one.

Of course he's entitled to one, the Divine said.

A gown was found for me, and the Divine and I

went back into the senior common room. I noticed that some fellows wore their gowns over jumpers and jeans.

The butler came in and opened the second of the double doors to the common room and announced that dinner was served. There was a printed menu:

Dinner

★

★   ★

Asparagus Spears
with
Parma Ham
Black & Green Olives
Vinaigrette Dressing

★   ★   ★

Salmon & Brill Plait
with
Ginger
Waldorf Salad
Parisienne Potatoes

★   ★   ★

Exotic Fruit Salad
&
Cream

★   ★   ★

Fresh Fruit and Stilton Cheese Available
Cairanne, Côtes du Rhônes Village,
Caves des Coteaux, DB, 1982
Macon Peronne, Du Mortier,
M. Josserand, DB, 1983

I saw, beyond the high table, the undergraduates carrying their cafeteria trays to and from the tables, and through the talk all about me I heard their distant voices and the sounds of their knives and forks against their plates.

After dinner, on my own, I went out into town to walk about until rain fell, and when I came into the college I saw an undergraduate standing in the front court, in the rain. He was still and he was staring out, I wondered at what. His long, loose hair was wet. I stopped and said, You'd better get in, you'll catch cold, and I said good night, and walked a little away, but I didn't want to leave him, so I went back and saw he was still standing in the rain and staring, I thought, into the universe.

My writing sessions were held around the dining-table in my set of rooms for those undergraduates who were interested.

I had a vision of writing that was against spluttering sausages on the grill, or the sickly green water in the glass vase of dead flowers, or the dust fluffs under the bed that rolled out slowly whenever the bed was made. The limitations of description, I tried to impress on my writers, was a limitation on a world of words, on the wonder of the writing itself. In the stories submitted to me there were lots of sputtering sausages, fluffs of dust, vases filled with rotting stems, all straining to describe the world lived in, as though that was all there was, and nothing more.

In my rooms and dressing for a college feast, I heard a knock on my door and I opened, and there he was, the beautiful undergraduate I had seen in the rain. I was in my pleated formal shirt, without trousers, trying to fit cuff links into my cuffs, fumbling.

Yes? I asked, my cuffs dangling.

I'm sorry, he said.

Nothing to be sorry about, I said, holding out an arm with the loose sleeve and in the other hand the cuff links. You can help me with these.

He hesitated.

Come along, I said, and, dear God, I watched him, frowning a little, insert each link – gold, oval, simple – into a cuff and secure it with the little mechanism at the end with the tips of his fingers, his hands, I noted, large and masculine for such a young man.

As he turned away from me, I saw his slender nape and fine hairs from the knot loose about it, and he turned back to look at me and then he turned away. But when I said, Come to tea tomorrow, he turned back and smiled.

There is no greater blessing than the smile of a beautiful young man.

He came to tea.

I asked him what he was reading, and he answered that he was reading classics.

He came to tea often, which was ordered from the pantry, with, yes, rounds of smoked salmon, cress, cucumber sandwiches, the butter thick.

The sunlight through a window on a Turkey rug.

And he, on the divan, and I in an armchair, he told me bits that he had discovered in his reading about the classics that amused him.

Ione of Chios knew of a letter beyond the alphabet, a letter that had no written sign, a letter used by Greeks and Latins, pronounced aggulus. What letter in what words this was used for was forgotten.

He was bright; he was spirited; he had wit; he was beautiful.

Another bit:

When, in Egypt, Thales learned many things, both philosophical and commercial, such as the Egyptians worshiped their Gods in the forms of beetles, serpents, hawks. And from the Egyptians he learned that if the right eye lid twitches, one will overcome one's enemies. If the lid of the left eye twitches, this in a free man means gain, but in a slave treachery. In a widow, this twitch means a voyage.

And one more:

Spartans leap into the air and, before descending, make complicated movements with their feet, called the

Tong dance, no one but a Spartan knows why.

It happened that after a tea he didn't put the tea things on a tray, as he always did, but went towards the door, where he stopped and he then turned back into the sitting room and sat on the divan.

I said I was sorry but I had to go to high table, as I had signed in. Hesitantly, he asked me if he could stay in my set while I was at high table. If he wanted, I said, if he wanted, but I was wary about leaving him on his own in my set, as I had no idea why he should want to stay there while I was away.

As high table, I sat next to the provost, who was a moral philosopher. No doubt the reader will assume I include my conversation with him in here for all the dimensions that it gives to my narrative, but, in fact, yes, I did ask the provost about philosophy, and it is an altogether valid dimension to the narrative that he should have said to me, We don't understand Plato, and that I should have asked, Why? and that he should have answered, Because Plato is poetry.

Returned from high table to my sitting room I found the undergraduate's shoes, but not him. I went into my bedroom and saw him on my bed, face up, the bedside lamp lit so the light shone on his forehead, cheeks, chin, lips. I approached the bed to lean over him to see that his chest rose and fell, and I knew from his breathing that he was not asleep.

I said, You'd better get up and go to your room.

45

He swung his legs to the edge of the bed and stood and he left me without saying good night. I went to the bedroom doorway and saw him in the sitting room put on his shoes, and I was about to call him back before he opened the door of my set and closed it after him. I returned to my room and I lay on the bed.

There are, the ancient Greek Philolaus of Tarentum wrote, desires that are stronger than ourselves.

Days later, I met the chaplain crossing the lawn.

He said he was concerned about my student, as the chaplain now considered him, though I did not give him tutorials so he was not my student.

Oh?

To integrate him into the college the chaplain had made him a member of a dining club.

And when the chaplain asked me if I would like to be invited to the club's dinner, I said, as I did when I was not sure of anything to say, Oh?

We all met at the train station in the bright evening, the women in black evening gowns, the men in black tie, the chaplain in his clerical collar. The chaplain introduced me to the ones I didn't know, and pointed to my undergraduate and said, You know each other, and we nodded. We waited on the station platform for the train.

I sat with the chaplain on the local, rattling train. No one else but our party was in the carriage, all the windows open to the countryside.

The chaplain said, I pray for him.

We passed through woods, the light slanting among the dark trees.

From the train station, our party walked in the continuing bright evening to a restaurant near the cathedral.

The private room above the restaurant was prepared for us.

The menu:

Tomato and Onion Soup
Smoked Mackerel

★

Chicken with cream and fresh herbs
Casserole of Pigeon

★

Choice of desserts

★

English cheeses

★

Coffee

And many bottles of house wine, red, of no particular vintage.

Whenever an elderly waitress came in with courses she was greeted with applause, which made her smile.

He sat at the far end of the table from me, and I tried not to look too long at him, but at moments we did look at each other, and for some long moments we held our looks, and then I felt at a great distance from him. But he talked with those about him, he smiled, he sometimes laughed.

Then the walk through the town, the streetlamps casting a level of yellowish light below the high level of the sky's silvery light, and the deserted streets. And the wait at the train station, no one else but our party there, even the ticket office closed; and the illuminated train arriving, and that, too, empty but for us.

And when, in the college courtyard, we disbanded, he walked away from me.

Perhaps because of the chaplain advising him, he no longer came to my rooms, but, in the foyer of a hall waiting for a piano recital to begin, I saw him leaning against a wall. I didn't wait for him to see me, but went to him, and when he did see me he smiled, and that smile was wide and beautiful in his face, more beautiful than when I had first seen him.

There were very few attending the recital, so, though he sat rows ahead of me, we appeared to be alone there together in such a large space, listening to the music.

During the slow movement of the piano sonata, I was attentive to every note as it occurred, slowly, slowly, slowly, so slowly that the tension as it increased would never be released, but which finally was released.

What is the too much in music that makes one think, I can't bear this?

He remained in his seat during the interval, and I kept to mine, so we were the only ones waiting in the hall, and that was all I could expect of him, that he would be in the same place as I was, his back to me, waiting during the interval for the pianist to return to the stage.

As we were both returning to the college, we walked together.

After hearing such music, there remains what awareness? You are walking beside someone who, you sense, is as aware of the music as you are, two people walking together, neither knowing why each is with the other, or where, really, they are going together?

In the college courtyard, I asked, would he like a cup of tea?

He said he would like that.

And the strange awareness of preparing the tea and drinking the tea.

I said, It's raining.

We went together to the window, on which rain was falling as though the deepening dark itself condensed into large drops that hit the pane.

Then one of those moments – one of those moments that has a long history but that is a-historical, that is personal but that rises high above the daily personal into the high bright impersonal, not a subjective appreciation, no, no, but somewhere where awareness is awareness of the universe – when, each of us leaning against the casements on either side of the window, we watched the rain fall outside.

And when I said, simply, the word rain, the word was resonant with more than the meaning of the word, and when he repeated, as if in another register, rain, I knew he meant more than the word.

He leaned his forehead against the windowpane, on the outside of which the rain fell and dripped down as though onto him.

I asked, You're listening to the rain?

He turned to me and smiled. He asked, The rain?

Aren't you listening to the rain?

No.

What, then?

He said, To music.

And he pressed his forehead to my chest.

There are no words to describe making love, none, and those that attempt to fail.

He fell asleep apart from me, wrapped in his side of the sheet, and I lay awake.

We write the word soul, but in what way, if no belief sustains the soul? Suspend judgment, and, at least in the writing and in the reading, too, give in to the pull of the word soul? Or believe outright? Dare to allow the expression its eternal fullness, and eliminate all that limits such fullness. Eliminate the furniture, the plates and cups, the pictures, the socks drying on the radiator, and allow the space as an essential in which the Gods appear.

They are the exiled Gods, the exiled Gods of long pasts, when they had sustained all the promises, promises that there would always be sunlight and rain, that there would always be fields of ripening wheat, that our temples would never fall into ruin.

This is what I thought as he slept beside me.

And what was there to say or do when, in the morning, I, still in bed, watched him, naked, dress in the clothes he had dropped to the floor, watched the hair under his arms expose the starkness of his nakedness when he raised his arms to draw on his undershirt over his mortal self? Dressed, he replaced the fallen pillow, and he raised the rumpled sheet to shake it out over me so it would be smooth, and for a moment, as the sheet descended on me, I was exposed in my slack nakedness, and when the sheet covered me he left.

I posted a note on my door that I would not have any writing sessions that day, though, in fact, fewer and fewer appeared, as if the reason for their having appeared had subsided into the demands of their tutorials.

I went to high table. Drunk, back in my bedroom, I undressed and got into bed and fell asleep, and when I heard a light knocking on the door to my set I thought it a sound in a dream that woke me. I raised my head to listen. There was another knock, lighter. Naked, I rose from the bed and went to the door and stood behind it, and I asked who was there, but no one answered. I opened the door a little to look out into the stark and illuminated passage, which was empty.

The chaplain came to tell me that the undergraduate had left the college, and had asked him, the chaplain, to say goodbye to me.

I read the Greek epigrams translated by him into English, which he had given to me, and which were a recourse to me:

> Here lies Saon of Acanthus, son of Dicon,
> who gave the gifts he could to the Gods,
> armloads of lilies, purple iris, roses,
> scattered in the rites for his dead son.

> I, Micylus, of a humble nature, pray that in my life
> I never made anyone unhappy, that the earth lie
> not too heavy on me, that the spirits
> don't lock me in darkness, for I did my best.

> I was a priestess of Demeter, first at Cabeiri, then at
> Dindymene, where I served the Goddess at her most vener-
> ated shrine.

> But I am now bones, I who succoured so many grieving
> wives who came to worship, who succoured, too, two sons in
> whose arms I died. Go on, passer-by, go on, and goodbye.

> Light-spirited when making love, Simone dedicated
> to Aphrodite a portrait of herself, a girdle
> men removed to kiss her breasts,

her torch for dark streets, and her magic wands.
Miccus cared for her lovingly in her old age,
his good nurse, and when she died
he had a statue of her carved in marble
to show her breasts, young and round with milk.

Traveller, rest here in the shade of a pine,
And listen to the distant flute of a shepherd
In the hills, and think that, in time,
You'll walk over the hills, and not return.

During Lent, I went every evening, on the sound of the bell, to the chapel for evensong, wearing the academic gown which allowed me to sit in the carved stalls, where the only other attendant was the Divine. Sometimes the chapel was almost empty, and freezing draughts blew through it. The few lit candles along the stalls made the chapel appear very empty. The choir came in, then the Lay Dean, and the chaplain, in the huge space, held the service. I especially liked the plainsong of the psalms, which I followed in a large, old psalter on a red velvet cushion stained with candle wax. The beater beat the measures, and the choir sang on and on.

Ash Wednesday, the chapel was crowded. The choir was in two parts, men and boys, at opposite ends of the chapel, with a soloist in the organ loft. And there was the beauty of the purity of the boys, their sexless voices rising and rising and never descending.

And then there was Easter.

There is no redemption, no, but there is during a church service. And then one left the church service, one left the chapel, one left the music. Still, one had been there.

My writing sessions came to an end.

In my rooms, I looked out of my open window at Webb's Court, filled with sunlit air. In the parterre, the buddleia — I think it was buddleia — was in full bloom. Someone from the pantry or buttery was wheeling a tea tray across the court; the dishes and cups rattled.

Everyone in the College was intent on work as Tripos neared. The grounds were shut to tourists most of the day. I saw the undergraduates emerging from their exams in tee shirts, shorts and sandals, into that sunlit air. And the May parties began.

I was invited by the Secretary of the Chetwynd Society to a garden party. The secretary hoped for much polite and earnest conversation, and promised the occasion would be most enjoyable. The neckties of the society were worn.

The Menu

★

Paté, French Bread, butter

★

York ham on the bone
Cold chicken

Salads

★

Strawberries, cream

★

Cheese

★

Fresh fruit

Jean Pericot Méthode Champenoise was to flow freely, at the cost of £0.75 per guest, a cheque for that amount, made out to the Secretary, to be left in his pigeonhole as soon as possible.

The secretary flitted from person to person, wanting to get everyone drunk on the cheap Spanish champagne – not really champagne – and worried because rain began to fall. Umbrellas were opened and some went for shelter in the entrances of Bodley stairways. The food, on long tables, was covered with white plastic tarpaulin in which water collected. Whenever the rain stopped, the closed umbrellas were stuck upside down in the lawn and everyone came out from the entrances, and everyone drank and when it rained again everyone remained in the rain, wet. The secretary went about groping all the men. A group of men gathered round him and lifted him, screaming, and, one two three, swung him back and forth.

I said to an undergraduate, I hope he can fly.

And he said, Of course he can fly. He's a fairy.

He was thrown into the Cam.

In my rooms, I looked out of my open window at the court below filled with sunlit air. In the parterre, the buddleia – I think it was buddleia – was in full bloom. Someone from the pantry or buttery was wheeling a tea tray across the court; the dishes and cups rattled.

Day after day was of totally clear sunlight, and I often left my writing to walk, sometimes alone, sometimes with others, in the countryside, where the ideals asserted themselves in densities of laburnum, lilac, broom; ideals kept unpretentious (nothing pretentiously cared for, natural, or seemingly so) by tangles of honeysuckle. And a walk through a little woods, the floor covered in bluebells, and out of the woods, along a path along the edge of a field high with cow parsley, in the distance a copse of chestnut trees in blossom, white and pink, and beyond the chestnut trees, on a low rise, the bright yellow of rape, and beyond that the clear pale blue sky.

And now, writing this, I write in the belief – though I know it is not a belief, but a desire I have that is stronger than any belief – that the world we live on is at the centre of the universe. This is not possible, but writing makes it possible.

Rock and Sunlight

He and I agreed that we would separate from each other after having lived together for twenty years, but before we did we also agreed that we would go on a last holiday together.

I had tender feelings towards him, as he was, between the two of us, the tender one.

Perhaps the only reason for our separating was my saying that an aging male couple, as we were, were not a pretty sight.

If that's the way you see us, he said.

In my mind, I stood away from us both together to see us, far from the beautiful youths we had been when we first met, as two aged men. How could there be between us now the attraction that the young are possessed by in one another, that attraction of young, vital, vivid bodies to one another, the attraction that discounts everything but itself, discounts even love?

Ah, yes, we had had that, we had been possessed by the naked bodies of each other, never, ever naked enough, even in the throes of naked sex, as if there was a deeper nakedness than the body that we were attracted to in each other, an essential nakedness more erotic than naked flesh, an essential nakedness that we had to possess in each other. That passion to possess had gone. I recognized that it had gone when I, incidentally, made my comment: we were not pretty as a couple.

Again, he said, If that's the way you see us.

I'll always have tender feelings for you, I said.

He smiled.

We decided to go on holiday to an island of sea and rock, and there, on flat rocks overlooking the sea, we lay side by side, naked, on towels, about us other naked people, men and women and children, lying, strolling about, diving off the rocks into the sea, all in the bright sunlight.

I lay back and closed my eyes and dozed, and when I opened my eyes I saw that my lover – my then ex-lover – was staring at the young man who had appeared and, naked, was lying near us; and as my almost ex-lover was staring at the sleek young man so was the young man staring at him.

I said, You're much too old for him.

Am I?

You are.

He doesn't seem to think so.

And my ex-lover rose and walked the few steps to where the young man lay and crouched down, so, his back to me, I saw his balls hanging down between his legs, to talk with the young man, who rose up on his elbows with a smile.

My ex came back to say he and the young man

would go off together for a walk, and he gathered up his clothes and towel and, smiling, he stood for a moment above me.

I said, You'll only be hurt.

You're the one who's already hurt by my going off with him.

Why should I be hurt? You and I are no longer together.

Still, you're hurt.

For fuck's sake, will you go off with him, go off? But don't come back to me crying because you've been hurt.

He got on his knees to lean towards to me to kiss me, but I turned away.

I said, Go, just go.

He went off with the young man, and, sorry to say, my tender feelings became hard.

I turned over onto my stomach, feeling my body pressed against the rock through my towel and I closed my eyes. I felt the sunlight on my bare back.

Rock and sunlight, I thought, rock and sunlight, rock and sunlight.

Reconciliation

Father and son were standing before a burning pile of leaves that the father had raked together.

The son said, I wish I didn't have to leave.

And I wish you didn't have to.

Can't you convince Mum that we can all stay together?

I've tried. You know I've tried.

Try again.

Your mother believes it is best that you go away with her, and her belief has more backing by the law than mine.

Who invented that law?

Oh, say history.

History?

History makes up laws then changes the laws, and history made up a law that your Mum loves you more than I do.

His son didn't understand. She loves me more than you do?

Well, let's say she loves me much less than she loves you, and presented all kinds of evidence to show that she had every reason not to love me at all.

Still not understanding, the boy looked at the flames

rising among the brown leaves. He frowned. But you do love me as much as she loves me.

That's true.

The boy asked, So we can't all live together again?

Not unless there is a reconciliation.

What's that?

Your Mum and I loving each other again, sort of anyway.

That's impossible?

It looks that way.

Can't there be a law that you both have to stay together?

Once, there was such a law.

History made such a law?

That's right – in history, past history, there was such a law.

And the law changed?

The law changed in history.

The leaves began to smolder, and with the thin-tyned rake the father turned them over and flames appeared among them again.

His son asked, Can history change again and make a law that we all have to stay together, all of us?

Is that what you want?

I do, yes, the boy said.

The father propped the top of the handle of the rake on his chin and thought:

Daddy, the boy said, I love you more than Mummy.

Save my son from love, save my darling son from loving this person, that person, the other person, all lawlessly, all irreconcilably.

Reason

In college, a Jesuit college, he was taught logic in his Freshman year in the belief that reasoning would set the syllogistic framework of all his thinking, not only in matters of reasoning up to the existence of God, but in matters of choosing his career, of marrying, of bringing up children, and of politics.

His wife told him she wanted a divorce. Why? he asked. Why? He didn't understand why the death of their son caused her to want to divorce him. No, she said, he didn't understand because there was no understanding of why. She needed to be alone; she felt she had no choice, but was compelled to go off on her own, far away if possible, and start another life. But she did have a choice, he said; everyone had choices. Hadn't she chosen to marry him? Hadn't she chosen, with him, to have a child? Why couldn't she choose to stay with him and together start another life, even to having another child, as they were still young enough? No, she said, no, the death of their son made her feel she had gone dead, she and her life with her husband, and the only possibility of life she felt she had was to be on her own, somewhere, oh, far away.

He pleaded with her to try to think her feelings

through, pleaded with her to use her power of reasoning, which she had, which he was sure she had.

She said, You reason for me; you tell me why I should stay married to you when all the feeling I have left of our marriage is that it's as dead as our son.

Feeling, he said, just feeling.

Yes, she retorted, feeling, feeling.

She saw she had hurt him, and she was sorry.

It's not your fault, she said, not your fault that he fell; and, too, you're the one who should feel most about his death, you're the one who went down to him and carried him up to me, just standing there; you're the one who should shock me for what you feel, more than I'm shocking you.

He said, How else do you think I can deal with the shock but to try to give his death some reason?

Tell me, she exclaimed, tell me, tell me, what reason? Give me a reason why our son is dead.

He closed his eyes and lowered his head as if to think, but he was weeping.

If only the reason was revealed to him, which he would reveal to her, for there had to be a reason, he was sure that there had to be a reason,

Even if he had not believed in God, the idea, in itself, the idea that death had to have some reason was to the glory of reason.

His wife did divorce him and did go far.

He was in politics, and he made choices in politics

that he did think out carefully before he made them.

He never could give up on reasoning.

Alone, most often lying in bed and unable to fall asleep, he would concentrate on what could possibly be the first principle on which all of reasoning would then be structured. Was the simplest, the essential preposition: he was alive? And might a second preposition be: to be alive was to know he was alive? Was this true? It was true to him. A third preposition followed, he thought, logically: the greater knowledge of life the greater the life. Or was this a faulty syllogism? No doubt it was, no doubt, but the reasoning seemed to him to justify the belief. Seemed? No, for him it did justify the belief. He would never, ever give up on the power of reasoning, never, ever give up trying to think his way up to the first principle, the essential, upon which reason developed a vision of life that gave sublime reason to life — for reason gave sublimity to the knowledge of life, which sublime knowledge made one want to live and live and live. And, yes, reason would give enrapturing reason to death, would, would, would, he knew, with all the faith he had in reasoning, give mortality reason in immortality. He believed, he believed: there was a reasoning beyond his reasoning, and all his impulse was to expand his soul out into that reasoning, and out there find fulfilment in peace.

The Setting Sun

He stood at a stone wall that was an edge to the dark valley where the lights of houses were like reflections of the stars. When he turned round to the square, he saw, in the diffused light of streetlamps, a girl walking towards him. She stopped for a moment at the wall not far from to look out over the valley – she was slim and pale and had a mass of thick black hair – then she walked away quickly.

He saw her again the next morning at breakfast in the hotel. He was traveling alone for the summer. Part of him wanted to be alone, and another part of him thought that, alone, he would be open to meet people. He had the feeling that the slim, pale girl, her hair massively disordered, was also traveling alone, and he glanced at her from time to time across the stark white room with square tables with plain white cloths. She wore a white cotton sleeveless dress, and her long, thin, bare arms appeared so pale the moles showed black.

He thought: She needs help.

Her shoulder bag was hanging by its strap over the back of her chair, and as she rose she put her arm through the strap, but the strap caught around a wooden knob at a corner of the backrest, and, instead of unlooping it, she yanked at it and the chair toppled sideways and crashed over onto the floor. She held her hands to her cheeks and wailed, and he jumped up to set the chair upright.

It's fine, he said. It's fine.

The girl picked up her bag and slipped the strap over her shoulder and said, Thanks, and again she placed her hands over her cheeks.

It really will be all right.

She smiled a weak smile.

He invited her to his table and they talked about where they'd been and where they planned to go. But she was uncertain, and thought she should go back home. No, no, he insisted, there was so much to see.

Come on, he said, I'll take you on a tour of the town.

She hesitated.

Come on.

Will you wait for me if I run up to my room for a minute to do my hair?

He waited in the small lobby. He'd done what he'd felt he had to do. He was always doing what he felt he had to do. He waited for a long time. She came down the stairs, her hair in a thick braid at her nape.

They went out into the heat to the main square and stood together before an ancient temple, with steep, yellowish-grey steps and dark, fluted, chipped columns and a soot dark pediment, squeezed in among medieval buildings. He told her the history of the temple. Blinking, she concentrated, or tried to.

With a little sigh, she said, Oh, I don't know.

He asked her if she'd like to sit at a café in the square. He was tall, and his blondish hair, longish because he had been too shy to go to a barber in a foreign place, hung in bangs over his eyebrows and he kept shoving it back. He shoved it back often while he and she sat in silence at the café.

The late morning sunlight glared on the old stone buildings, and the heat seemed to come as much from the stone as from the sky. All the hill town was hot, shuttered, and here and there, crammed among the stony walls, were galleries with pictures to study, churches to visit, ruins to contemplate. He hadn't realized how tired he was of touring. Looking into dark doorways, walking up steep, wheel-rutted, paved streets, climbing stone stairs to the carved, arched bays about church doors, following the pillars along porticos, descending spiral staircases into low crypts, passing from sunlight into shadow, from shadow into sunlight, was, in a way, like thinking, and he was thinking too much.

They ate dinner together in the hotel restaurant. Their rooms were next to one another.

He couldn't sleep. He heard the squeal of her bed springs from behind the wall. He got up, went to the little sink in a corner, turned on the tap and peed. Back in bed, he heard her walking around her room.

When, in the morning, he heard her close the door to her room and walk along the corridor past his room, he thought he, too, had to go out and down to the restaurant to join her, though he didn't want to. He didn't want to see her again. But he joined her with a wide smile.

She had un-braided her hair, which looked as though she had combed it out with her fingers, and she looked paler than before.

From time to time during the day, he made excuses to leave her, such as excusing himself to go to the men's room though he didn't need one, and after their simple lunch he suggested that they rest until the evening. She agreed. She didn't ask for anything, but he felt, more and more, that he had to give her everything. They met again in the late afternoon.

He felt that he would be with her for the rest of his life, and he would try, he would try, to love her, because she needed love.

The Two Selves

I was at a party, where I drank too much and, drunk, was more expansive in my talk and gestures and laughter than I'd been with my lover, who had died a month before – as if I, who'd survived, had been liberated.

A close friend said to me, You're beyond love.

Where am I, then? I asked.

You don't know?

I don't know.

And I suddenly felt I died, and I looked at the self who was alive and drunk and almost rowdy, and I thought: he is a fool.

If that foolish self was beyond love, he was where love wasn't possible.

My dead self withdrew, went outside alone – out into the rain – and, still and silent, that self tried at least not to judge the foolish self he had left behind in the party. He must go home, the home he continued to live in since the death of his lover three years before. But he waited until his close friend came out, as he knew his friend would.

I wish you wouldn't withdraw.

I can't help myself.

You can help yourself. You should by now have got

over your grief. Your withdrawing the way you do, so everyone sees you go out, looks like an affectation.

An affectation?

Yourself the drunken one, flirting with the boys – that's you as you really want to be, that's you sincere.

That's me a fool.

You're being a fool now. Let's go inside and have a drink. The boy you were flirting with, he asked where you'd gone to, and I said I'd fetch you back to him.

I think not.

Come along. It's raining, if you hadn't noted.

No. No, thanks.

Perhaps I was affected, because, yes, I did want everyone to know, when grief overcame me so I went dead, that my grief was so great I must withdraw, but withdraw so that everyone else saw me withdraw. And, yes, I expected someone to come out to bring me back into the party, where my friends, or even a boy, would cheer me up and I would become the out-going self. But what no one understood was that it was only as the grieving inner self that I knew love. The outer self didn't.

But I went back into the party with the host, who brought me together with the boy he said I'd been flirting with.

He had about his head a garland of flowers which I took off and placed on my head.

Be the fool, I told myself, go on, be the fool.

The Smell of Honeysuckle

The two of us, old friends, were having supper on the terrace. Often, as if this were part of the ease of our being old friends, we became silent and sat back in our chairs and looked out and away from each other.

The air in the hot evening smelled of the honeysuckle growing on a trellis along the sides of the terrace.

I sat forward and poured wine into the empty glass she held out for me. Her hand was shaking so, the wine spilled a little over the rim.

But she closed her eyes and her breathing sounded in the stillness.

She said, How peaceful.

How very peaceful, I said.

You know, I think I am, finally, at peace.

I'm glad for you, I said, I'm very glad for you, very glad.

It's taken time to find peace, she said. After my divorce, I thought I would never have him back, ever, given what he'd done to me. Yes, I had the villa, but even then I thought he hadn't gone far enough when I heard he'd rented an apartment in town, because I wanted him to go far away. If I happened to be in town and we met in the street by accident, I nodded, but that was all, I just nodded. Why I had him back when he became ill, I don't know. Why I let him sleep with me, I don't know. And I don't know why, when he became so ill he couldn't leave the bed, I cared for him. And, I'll tell you, when I woke up at dawn and found him dead beside me, I loved him, I really and truly don't know why I loved him when he was dead.

I said, quietly, You wouldn't keep asking yourself why if you were really over him.

The way you got over – but she stopped, because she thought I wouldn't want to be reminded of my past, which neither of us wanted to be reminded of.

Never mind. Smell the honeysuckle.

She raised her chin to breathe in the smell, then she said with sigh, Oh, what we have to get over, so much, so much, and so much of it about feelings that we don't want to come back to us. It shouldn't, I know it shouldn't, but the feeling I had when I found him dead beside me, the love I suddenly felt for him, that keeps coming back to me, and I can't get over that. Her glass held up for more wine, she said, No, I can't get over that.

Hold your glass still, I said.

Singing the Universal World

She was looking out of the wide windows of the recital hall onto the river below when the bell rang for the second half of the programme, but she stood a little longer at the window, looking at the river, and when the bell stopped ringing she hurried to her seat.

The soprano, in a long, silver and white gown, stood at the curve of the piano, her hands folded at her waist. The spotlight about her and the pianist and the piano appeared to expand a little and to carry them off as the soprano sang:

Schöne Welt, wo bist du?

She wanted very much to learn this song to be able to sing it, for herself.

The sky was still light when the recital ended. Outside the hall, she felt she was wandering she wasn't quite sure where, and when she found herself crossing a bridge over the river she wondered how she got there.

Towards the middle of the bridge a man was standing at the railing, holding to it, looking down at the river flowing dark and fast below. The man was tall, with a wide, pale face. She didn't like the way the man was staring down at the river. As she passed him, he turned to look at her for moment, but long enough for her to see that the veins in his eyes were broken. She passed him, but at the other end of the bridge she turned back to see the man was again staring down into the river. Tentatively, she approached him, and he again turned to her and, as if frightened of what she would do to him, he hurried away. She hurried after him, but stopped when she saw him, once again turn to her with a look of terror on his face, then stumble down from the bridge to the embankment. She now held to the rail and stared down at the river, which ran in deep, dark, infolding currents.

She heard someone ask, Are you all right?

She opened hr eyes and looked back to an elderly man in a black, pinstripe suit and a bowler hat.

I'm quite all right, she said.

A dizzy spell?

Something like that.

The man nodded and left, and she remained where she was, clutching for a long whole before releasing her grip to go on across the bridge.

She walked slowly through the city she knew well, the city she was born and brought up in. The streets appeared lit from the sky, not from the streetlamps, and young people moved in loud groups along the pavements. In the square with a fountain, young people were gathered, and cars, with white headlamps and red taillights pale in the late afterglow of the sun, curved round the crowd. The young people separated to let her pass among them, and even in the narrow streets of the business quarter of the city, the young people were gathered on the pavements outside pubs, drinking, their half-filled glasses of lager poised on the stoops of entrances to nearby office buildings, and they too drew back, smiling, to let her pass. In her residential quarter, she heard from behind the hedges of locked, private gardens in the squares, voices and soft laughter. The air was moist.

From across a square and through the dark trees in the garden square, she saw the house in which she had a flat, the windows dark.

Sleep

She was very ill, but she said she would fight her illness, would fight the cancer as if the cancer were a dark body within her body that was stronger than her outer body and that would take her over; she would fight back, day after day, by countering that inside dark body with all the bright pleasures of seeing, of hearing, of tasting, of smelling, and, yes, of touching. Not that she was extravagant in indulging her senses; no, she was never extravagant, was, ill as she was, always calm, as if the most acute of sensations needed her to be calm to be attentive to them.

She asked me, her lover, if we could take a trip together, just for a week, because she thought that in a foreign place she would be all the more attentive to everything because unfamiliar to her. I said, yes, yes, of course. She chose a small, walled in town, medieval, and there, settled in a modest hotel in a narrow street between the high brick façades of medieval palaces, I followed her around, she with her guide book, into churches, where she stopped to examine carefully such details as delicately painted fruit, or the drape of a robe, or the pattern on a marble floor (she was particularly attentive to details), or into the ecclesiastical museum attached to the church where ceremonial vestments embroidered with gold hung in glass cases with the finely worked vessels of worship; and, yes, there was a recital of chamber music in the town's opera house, which we attended, the music played by students from the town's music school, not well, in fact badly, but she would raise a finger to indicate a passage that she thought had a lilt; and of course there was the restaurant where she examined the menu carefully, and, with knowledge enough in the language, chose the specialty, which was a stew of fish and crustaceans in a tomato sauce, and she chose the wine; and then we walked the narrow streets to where we came to a flight of steep streets, and I noted that she took the steps one at a time, pausing often, I with her.

Go ahead, she said, as if she was annoyed by my solicitousness, and I did climb with a lively step up to the top, from where, between the spaces of the buildings, the landscape of valleys and mountains made me imagine that the square and the buildings and the façade of the church floated among the valleys and mountains. I watched her, below, climb the steps, and I thought, She is determined, and she will make it, because, as easy as she appears to be, I know her will power. I held out my hand to her to climb the last step, and she took it, and I saw in her face, now pale, that the fight was over.

There, on a stone bench in the square, we sat for a long time, silent, looking out at the valleys and mountains seem to become more and more distant as the light faded.

She said, We'd better get back.

Back was down the many flights of stone steps to where, on my asking, there was only a bus to take us to the town where we had our hotel room. In a café, we waited until dark for the bus.

On the bus, she sat up straight, her eyes closed.

I wished, in our hotel room, that we were in our bedroom, in our home, in a place that was familiar to us, and where we had our doctor.

She did not want me to try to have a local doctor come.

A doctor won't be able to help, she said.

In bed with her, I, awake, waited for her to fall asleep, and when she was asleep, I thought, there is nothing more sublime in love than lying awake next to your lover and watching your lover sleep.

Weather

A sultry evening, stilled, the air redolent of pine trees and of mist rising from the warm lake, in the distance frogs talking with crickets, and we five friends sitting in a circle out on the lawn, the only light projected from the windows of the large field-stone house where we were staying for a long weekend.

Here, nothing mattered but that we were all friends speaking in our different voices.

One of us said, listen, out on the lake, the sound of splashing oars.

We listened.

The boat is being rowed away from us.

We listened until the sound of the oars clanking in the oar locks came from further and further away, became silence.

And here, as the writer of this story, I become aware of a difficulty that all writers face, which is to introduce into the setting meaningful talk, if meaningful has to do, as in this story, with the subject of love. There is a way of doing this, which is to make the setting so particular that the conversation becomes, itself, as particular as the setting, and could not have occurred anywhere there, where someone was rowing a boat out on the misty lake.

I stood and stretched my arms out wide and breathed in deeply the air, and then, I didn't know why, I walked away to where the sloping lawn gave way to the darkness of the lake. In the light from the windows I walked down to the dock, and stood and stretched out my arms again and again breathed in deeply, the air here with a faint smell of fish. A row boat was moored at the dock, and, still without knowing why, I freed the boat from its moorings and got in and rowed out onto the lake, the oars in the oar locks clanking as I rowed out far. I knew I was not absenting myself from the conversation because I thought it embarrassingly simplistic for adults to indulge in; no, I in fact thought it profound, and out on the lake thought carefully about what had been said. Out far enough to see the lights of the house, I let the boat drift. My friends must have assumed that I, perhaps embarrassed by the conversation, had left them and gone to my room. I would tell them, the next day, that I'd left because I needed to carry away with me the immensity of the questions raised, as if I couldn't have sustained a greater immensity. I saw the lights of the house go out, one after another, as my friends went to their rooms and to bed.

Strange Signals

In the museum of fine arts, he studied, in glass cases, vases and unfurled scrolls and porcelain figures that had been collected by the old families of the city and bequeathed to the museum, the city he was born and brought up in, with its old commons and brick houses on a hill and at the top of the hill a state house with a gold dome.

Studying the objects, he thought there was something he wanted to understand, something strange, in the way his mind, straining to understand, suddenly found release in a vase, the white vase calligraphed in black.

He was a young man in a blue shirt with a button-down collar and wearing brown buckskin shoes, in his sophomore year at college.

He left the museum and walked through the fens, where he passed high, thick rushes growing around a pond. The rushes were moving as if someone were within the rushes and moving, and he stopped.

He stepped back, but then he hesitantly stepped a little closer to the reeds, and, as if seeing himself from a long distance, he stepped even closer to where the reeds opened and he saw a lean hand emerge and signal to him.

God help me, he thought.

And he hurried away, out of the fens and along pavements with cars passing by him.

A hand had signalled something, and whatever it had signalled was frighteningly strange to him.

He was intelligent, he was imaginative, and he believed in God, because the greatest strangeness was the strangeness of God, who kept sending signals to him.

God made signals with a lace handkerchief, a glove, a boot, and in God's silence the sound of a plucked violin on a Sunday winter afternoon after the meeting in the meeting house and the walk back in the snow.

And when he thought of God, he thought of a table set with pewter plates that kept the cloth in place, and no one in the room.

He thought of waking on a cold morning to see snow outside, snow that had drifted against the barn, the air now still and bright. He saw himself with a man and woman in simple black on their way through the snow to the meeting house with its plain wood and clear windows, there where he saw himself, alone, cold, the shadows as long as pews, and the pulpit waiting for the preacher to stand and read from the big black book, and he, head bowed, devoted to the shadows before the lights were lit, to the silence before the sermon.

The Fall

After reading *Deep-Holes* by Alice Munro

She was a widow with a son. He was home for the summer from college, and he was restless, but as restless as he was he did not want to do anything, not see friends, not read the books assigned to him, not even ride his bicycle along the country lanes as he did when he was a boy. He stayed at home, and this worried his mother, made her wonder what was going on in him, for he hardly spoke, and then only to say, No, no, he didn't feel like it, to whatever she proposed to – as she thought – get him out of himself.

She proposed a picnic. He didn't say no. She elaborated her proposal hoping he would say yes: they'd go to the gorge and have their picnic, just the two of them, down by the river that flowed through the gorge. He surprised her by saying, Yes, he'd like that, he hadn't been there in so long, and he wanted once again to look out at the view from the top of the gorge.

Ah, she remembered, she said, how he did love views, and it came to her that what he needed was just that: to look out beyond himself, far out beyond himself.

At the top of the path that led steeply down the side of the gorge, she waited, the picnic basket at her feet, for her son to go up to a higher point, a rocky promontory, for the view he had come to look out at. She watched him stand there, then, from a lower vantage, she too looked out at mountains falling and rising to always higher mountains. When she looked back to see watch him on that high rock, he was not there. The shock was that he had never been there, that she had imagined he had been there, and that she was alone, absurdly alone in a place where she had no reason to be alone, a picnic basket at her feet. Alone as she was, she ran up to the rock and looked down to where her son lay below, face up, his legs bent in ways that legs do not bend, and he was still. She felt so alone, there could not have been anyone to help her, and when she screamed she was surprised that a man appeared near her, and another man and woman. The woman held her and turned her away from the precipice as though to hold her back from falling, and the men rushed off for the help she was incapable of.

Her son was alive, but the bones of his legs were shattered, and he would be a cripple.

What she thought she would never know, because she would not ask him and he would not tell her, was: had he thrown himself from the rock?

She nursed him during his long convalescence. His restlessness went, and as he lay in traction he seemed to be relieved that nothing was demanded of him. When she said the college he attended would of course have him back on his recovery, he said, aggressively, he wouldn't go back – no, he wouldn't go to college, wouldn't confine himself to what was expected of him by the world he was brought up in.

Surprised, she asked, what world was he brought up in?

He answered, The world where everything depends on I, I, I, I, and what I did, what I succeeded in, what I won at. What he wanted was to give up being I and everything that I called for, as if I were the centre of the world. He was not the centre of the world, and he would do whatever he could not to be the centre.

She didn't understand.

No, she wouldn't, she only ever thought about herself, like everyone else.

She drew back into herself, astonished. How could he say that she only ever thought about herself after everything she had done, was doing, would go on doing for him, from his birth? How could he deny her being a loving mother to him?

Then he accused her, and his accusation made her draw back more into herself: She didn't know what love was, not really; love wasn't loving just another person, love opened you out to everyone.

What did he mean? she asked.

Again, she wouldn't understand.

Try me, she said; at least try me.

Can you understand that I don't love anyone, but

that I do love everyone? Can you understand that I don't care that you're my mother, that I'm your son? Can you understand that I don't care that my father was my father, that I was his son? What I care about is, oh, greater, much greater.

This sounds as if you've taken up religion.

Strange to you, he said, not to me; and if it's a religion then I'm devoted.

That was the last full conversation she had with him while he lived with her.

And when he was able, using crutches, he left her. She watched him from the open doorway go out with only a small bag, she had no idea where to. He did allow her to give him money; and he did allow her to hug him before he went out to a car waiting at the curb, though she did not know who was waiting for him in the car or how he had contacted the person waiting for him in the car. Perhaps the person was a member of the religion her son was devoted to. She saw her son manoeuvre his crutches to get into the car, and she watched the car go off. Shutting the front door, she was too stunned to feel anything, and her only thought was: let him go, let him go.

Let her son go?

She remarried, she had another child, another son. With the baby son in bed between her and her husband, she said she wished she knew where her grown up son was, just that, just to find out if he was all right. Her husband suggested getting the police to find out. No, no, she said, and she realized she didn't want to know. She had let that son go.

The local newspaper reported a fire that had burnt down a large tenement in the slums of the city, and with the report was a photograph, and in the photograph she recognized her son – yes, it was him, it had to be him, though now without crutches – helping an old lady out of the building. Smoke was billowing out of the windows. She laid the paper down. So he was in the city she lived in, and he was, no doubt, a member of the religion – she corrected herself: call it a cult – that helped people out of burning buildings, helped people who needed help. Some tension in her gave way, tension she hadn't been aware of since he had left her, five years before; and she sat back with at least the assurance that he was among good people. Good people?

But she – wasn't she good? His accusation came back to her with a pang: that she didn't know what love was. She wanted, now, right now, to confront him with the fact: she did know what love really was. She had loved him. What she should have felt at the time of the accusation she felt impelled to do now: to shout out to him that loving everyone was loving no one. What did he – what did the people of his cult – know about loving another, day by day, month by month, year by year, one I having to accommodate to another I, one I having to compromise with another I, one I having to forgive another I? It was easy to save an old woman from a burning building, but try living with that woman and loving her. After all these years, she wanted to see him, face to face, she wanted to tell him what she should have told him: that he had sinned against his mother by accusing her of not loving him.

She went to see the tenement building. Only the windows of top floor were burned out, the shingles about them black. The front door was off so she saw into the entry, where there was a baby's buggy. People were living in the lower floors. One came out and sat on the stoop before the door-less entry.

Shivering, though the day was hot, she walked about the slums, her small purse held tightly against her breasts, knowing that her son was there in the slums.

And there he was, standing alone on the stone steps of an abandoned bank. He had a beard and his hair was long, but she recognized his smile, for he did smile when he recognized her. Without crutches, but with staggering movements of his body, he descended the steps towards her. She waited, shivering more.

He said, Hello. He had missing teeth, and his face was haggard.

Hello, she repeated.

She was shivering, but her voice was calm.

He said, Come with me.

She followed him to an almost derelict brick building, this, too, without a front door. The front door had been broken into so many times, he said, the people living in the house decided to take it off so everyone could enter who wanted to, knowing there was nothing inside to steal.

Who is living in the house? she asked.

Anyone who wants to.

He led her into a kitchen where, before an old fashioned range, a large woman, her back to them, was stirring the contents of a large pot.

He asked, How's it going?

She turned a distorted face to him and then turned away.

His room was downstairs, in the basement, the walls so damp the wallpaper patterned with roses was loose.

His narrow bed had on it an old army blanket with burn holes.

Sit on the bed, he said.

She did, and he sat next to her.

Well, he said.

I'm glad to see you don't have to use crutches any longer.

Practice.

She asked, Do you ever think of your father?

No, never.

Nor, I suppose, do you think of me.

Only when I need money, but then I would never ask, as I have never asked.

I can give you money.

And I'll take it.

But what do you use the money for?

Drugs.

Drugs?

Yes, drugs.

I thought you might use the money for, oh, altruistic reasons.

Because you saw a photograph of me helping an old woman out of a burning building?

That, and because of what you once said.

What did I say?

That I don't know what love is, but that you do.

Did I say that?

Instead of answering, she opened her purse and took out a sheaf of bills, as if ready for her to hand to him, which she did, and, taking the sheaf, he thanked her.

Why did you help the old lady from the burning building?

I don't know why.

You must have wondered after the fact.

I don't wonder. I just do, just that, I just do.

You don't belong to a cult?

I did, I suppose I did, helping people who needed help. But you can't help people. There are too many people, too many, that need to be helped. There's a whole world of people who need to be helped, and no help will make that world any smaller. It gets bigger and bigger and bigger, the world of all the helpless people.

There is helping one other person.

Such as you're helping me, your son.

She stared at her son.

He said, I can't be helped. I don't want to be helped. I've seen enough of helplessness that I know there is no help, none, not for me or for you or for anyone.

You make me angry, your saying that. You made me very angry when you accused me of not loving you. You don't know anything about love. Why I wanted to see you – I wanted to tell you that, I wanted and I want to tell you that, I did love you, I did, I did.

She swung out and hit him across his face, and, for a moment startled, he smiled.

He said, You didn't love me enough. You can't love enough, you'll never be able to love enough, no one can or will be able to love enough. Listen to me, listen to your son: I've seen the worst, seen people no one can love, and once I did try to help those people, for the sake of love, for that great beaming light of love that loves us all. You'll call it a cult belief, so, yes, a cult belief. I failed. I failed. I failed. I tried to sustain love for the loveless. I couldn't do it. And now I do, day by day, I just do; I just do and I don't wonder at what I do.

Did you throw yourself off that rock?

He stood.

I did, yes I did. Again, you won't understand. I myself can't understand. If you want to know the only love I was really capable of, it was there, when I threw myself out into space out of love, out of love that I felt was itself space that would hold me, and I would become space, become nothing but space.

He held out his arms.

You can't feel what I did feel, there, felt that if I let myself go, let go totally, let go even to throwing myself out into space, I would cease being myself and become, oh, all love.

My son, she thought; my son, my helpless son.

Lowering his arms, her son said, but I fell.

The Metaphor

Many years later I learned that a lover I had once spent nights with in his bed, in Rome, was dead, and I searched for a way to make sense of this, that someone I had made love with when we were both young was dead, and I thought that there had to be some sense in this, that in the throes of sex the Tiber had carried us out to where sea waves rolled us over and over and further and further out, and we let go, the sense now a memory charged with metaphor, as memory tends to be, all that I recall of him is his bed in a sunlit room, in Rome.

The Canoe

They were talking about a pine tree in the woods that was struck by lightning.

Father and son were on the screened-in porch, the screens seething with a warm breeze from the lake, then his son, saying nothing, went out through the screen door, and his father accepted that his son could walk off, after a silence between the two, to go he had no idea where.

Then he went out and down the rough path to where there was a narrow beach, and he sat on a bench made of a thick plank supported on rocks. The breeze caused low, long waves on the lake,

Once, his son had expressed the loose idea of becoming a priest, and this his father thought was one with his many loose ideas, but, again, no mention was made of the idea.

As the sun set a stillness spread over the lake, and a faint mist rose from the stillness, and fish broke the stillness in widening circles, the widening circles, he thought, of immortality.

He saw a canoe out on the lake, gliding towards the far shore. He was sure his son was in the canoe, which, from time to time, he let drift.

He stood, his behind aching from sitting on the bench. He was a man with short, bristling, grey hair, and in the shadows his face appeared gaunt. He slowly climbed the path from the lake to the house, and as he passed the woods that began where the path ended, he stood back when he saw his neighbour, a girl, standing among the trees.

She was wearing a loose white shift and she was barefoot, and her slender arms and legs were bare. She had walked through the woods on a path to come, she said, to visit, and she was just about to return to her parents' house when she saw him. She followed him to the door of the porch, but stood outside when he went in and switched on a light. He held the door open for her, but she didn't enter.

Did you see the pine tree that was struck by lightning? she asked.

No, but I think I saw the flash.

I saw it too.

She was a simple girl, perhaps simple-minded, whose parents were among the few old generations who lived around the lake, parents who might have been considered poor trash, if they were considered at all by the people from the city who had built houses on the lake.

The lightning cracked the trunk of the tree right down the middle, she said. It was that strong.

I guess it had to be that strong to crack the tree right down the middle.

Hesitantly, the girl asked, is he around?

He's out in his canoe.

I was just wondering.

She was, she knew, soft on his son, in her simple way.

He said, why don't you come in and wait for him? I'm sure he'd like to see you.

Oh, I don't know.

Sure, he will. He likes you. He likes you a lot.

Appeal

Their daughter was in prison, in another country, convicted of murder. This, they kept telling themselves, was impossible; their daughter was incapable of any act of violence, and certainly not murder, certainly not capable of clutching a knife with her accomplice – a man who picked her up in a train station of the provincial town, a man she had sex with in ways that her parents had never imagined – to stab in the neck a girl they had picked up together in the train station, stab her aorta so they were both covered in blood by the gush from the wound. Her parents heard this evidence, through a translator, but believed the translator had misinterpreted the event.

If their daughter took drugs, which, yes, they knew about, sort of, the drugs were mild, and not the drugs that made her crazy, so crazy that she would, as she herself admitted, feel that murdering a girl that her lover had raped in front of her, raped while she herself held the girl, naked, with her arms twisted behind her while he forced himself into her, feel love as she had never before felt it, the love of life. They saw their daughter in the witness box, with almost a smile, confess not only to the rape and murder but to going out with her lover after to a restaurant, for a walk in the old town, for a rock concert, and, too, their sex in the room where the girl lay dead, the bed soaked in blood. She was sentenced to life imprisonment, their daughter.

They would appeal, they would sell everything they had, their very home, to overturn the judgment.

The mayor of the town, from where the murder caused a world-wide scandal, was kind to the parents. He advised them not to put their own lives at financial risk for a judgment that could not be overturned, for their daughter, their daughter and her rough partner, had admitted to the crime.

Their daughter was refined, was blonde and delicately featured.

Could her partner – no, not her lover, not that – could her partner be persuaded to take on the responsibility, could he be persuaded that, given he, a foreigner in the country who already had a criminal record, would take all the blame for the act, their daughter only a witness?

The mayor looked at them sadly.

In their hotel room they tried to calculate how much money they were able to raise for the appeal. However they calculated, including borrowing, they knew they could not raise enough.

Still, they must appeal, they must. Appeal to whom, if they themselves could not support the appeal? Who would listen to them, who would believe their daughter was not guilty, who wouldn't feel that in some way they themselves were guilty in the way they had brought up their daughter?

What had they done wrong? What?

Standing together, they looked out of the window of the hotel room, down into a square where people were walking about in the illumination of street lamps with glowing globes, the illumination casting shadows of trees on the cobbles.

If only all this had happened in their own country, where they would at least have understood the language. But how could they return to their town?

He put an arm across her shoulders and they turned away from the window.

In whatever way, they would appeal, they would appeal and appeal and appeal, appeal by lowering themselves to kneeling and begging for mercy, because they loved their daughter.

Civilization

I was with him to try to console him, but he was close to hysteria.

Civilization? What is civilization? he asked, his voice high. Is this too basic a question to ask? We like to think that the art left by a past civilization is an indication of how high the civilization was – that fragments of frescoes of dolphins, of blue monkeys and partridges and hoopoes are proof of the spiritedness of the people, of politeness of manners and charm, of civility in the streets and justice in the rulers. And we like to think, too, that any discovery among the ruins of even shards of pottery from foreign places, evidence of trade, means an outward-looking civilization, always a good sign of accommodating to different points of view, perhaps even meaning peace with other civilizations. And when tombs reveal bronze swords with alabaster pommels, ivory-handled bronze daggers, the remains of a leather scabbard in gold appliqué, vases in silver and bronze, jewellery, earrings and diadems in silver and gold, and, indicating foreign contacts, a scarab in lapis lazuli, we assume that this high regard for the dead is a high regard for civilization.

But what about Sparta? he asked, his voice rising higher and higher, so he was sighing. Was Sparta not a civilization for leaving no evidence of poetry, of music, of statues, not even of eulogies for the dead? What is left of Sparta to be shown in a glass case in a museum? Surely, in Sparta there were rebels against the totalitarian city-state, and I would have been among those foolish few who had heard of Athenian freedom of expression and tried to speak out as an individual – perhaps – and here he laughed an hysterical laugh – tried to write a poem – then dealt with in whatever harsh way the Spartans would have dealt with rebels, most likely by killing them. Yet I will use the word 'Spartan' in praise of someone who is courageous in his devotion to an impersonal cause, a devotion inspired by his belief in the highest vision of his civilization. How could one not praise the Spartans at Thermopylae, fighting to the death for a totalitarian civilization without art, a civilization you and I would rebel against?

He paced about the room, which he refused to leave, pulling at his hair, his cheeks. The light in the room gave way to darkness, and with the darkness he became truly hysterical. I lit a small lamp. All I could do, I thought, was be with him.

Oh yes, he cried, an austere, totalitarian military state was Sparta, but dance was allowed, dance was allowed as an expression of what couldn't be disciplined – passionate dance, the dancers wearing grotesque terracotta masks to show that the undisciplined, passionate dancing was grotesque.

And I believe that all expression should be made through a mask, all, all, all — even grief, especially grief, expressed through a grotesque mask of an exaggerated grimace, of huge false tears falling down nail-torn, gouged cheeks. Especially grief.

His face was wet with tears and his cheeks were scored red.

Especially grief, he cried out, especially grief.

Order and Disorder

My son was about to go off to school, his first year and the first time he would be away from me for a long while.

His mother had died before he was able to remember her.

He said, I wonder who my roommate will be.

Whoever he is, I said, be good to him.

He nodded. He had a slender face and a slender neck, and I worried about his physical and spiritual delicacy. His smile was delicate.

I met his roommate when I brought him to his room, his roommate a young man with a broad, blond face and a broad smile. His body, too, was broad.

And when I left them together I walked about the campus on my own, in tears.

For my roommate, twenty years before in the same college, had killed himself.

Whenever I was in our room, he seemed, as if weak, incapable of doing anything more than lie on his bed and stare out.

Once, lying still while I, on the other side of the room, sat at my desk to write, I heard a slight wail from him. I thought he was asleep, and, sensing he must be cold, I covered him with my overcoat. Whether or not he'd been asleep, I didn't know; he opened his eyes and looked at me with such longing that I drew back. I had no idea what his longing was for. Perhaps the longing was, at the deepest, the longing to die. I drew back, but remained standing above him, and he smiled at me, and something moved in me.

One knows there is a soul when the soul moves, and a certain disorder confuses one's essential need for order.

Frightened of the disorder he caused in me, I stayed away from our room most of the day, in a corner of the library, and returned to our room after the evening meal when he was already in bed. More than before, I was orderly in my studies, in all the activities of the college. I was certain he did not go to classes, did not study, and would flunk out. On my return to our room, I would not switch on a light because I did not want to wake him for fear of what he might ask of me, if in fact he was asleep.

He woke me one night by sitting on the edge of my narrow bed, just across the narrow room from his. He leaned close and I became rigid, and all the more rigid when he lay on me, lay on me and pressed his face into the side of my neck.

I noted, beyond us, the window of our room, star-lit.

Disaster, I thought, is derived from *astres* with the prefix *dis*, and this meant a confusion among the stars.

With a sudden, almost involuntary jerk of my body I threw him off me, so he fell onto the floor. Pushing the bed clothes away, I sat up, but could only watch him struggle awkwardly to rise to his feet, his hands to his head. I'm sorry, he said, I'm so sorry, I'm so, so, so sorry, and he returned to his bed and fell onto the rumpled bed clothes.

As though in the immense confusion of the stars all about us, I stood and went to his bed and sat on the edge of his bed and said, I can't, I can't.

He touched my cheek and said, I know you can't.

My soul was in great confusion.

Did he kill himself – drowned himself in the pond at the bottom of the hill below the campus – because I could not return his love? There were other reasons, deeper reasons, but, oh, I felt – in my egoism I felt – that he had died of love for me.

And I have felt, all my life that I have never been able to return with equal openness the love that has been opened to me, though I have tried, though I have tried. The love of that roommate, the love of my wife, the love of my son, the love of so many others, love I have been so aware of not being able to return, all that love has been far in excess of the love I have been capable of. Love for me must rely on order, but love is all disorder.

Proof of the Existence of the Mother of God

She had wild hair, which appeared to rise on the shock of her drunken preaching. But her friends were used to her drunken preaching, and were amused, somewhat. We were at a summer garden party.

She said, Listen, listen.

Pitying her, I was the only one who listened.

She raised her glass.

Do you know anything about the ritual of ordination of priests?

Not really.

The ritual of ordination of priests is supposed to be a rebirth, a rebirth that eliminates women, as if men were reborn by men into the holiest presence of God. There it is: men are ritualistically reborn by men into new and holy lives, leaving behind their natural births by their mothers.

She held out her glass to me and asked for a refill, and I refilled her glass.

The bottles of wine were on a cloth-covered table, the white cloth stained with wine.

Not thanking me, she took her glass and said, God comes most naturally from the mother, from the very breast. The proof of the existence of God is not in the head, but in the breast. The high priest of the ordination of men into the holiest presence of God should be – has to be – a woman, who gives birth to men and in giving birth passes on the nature of true religion, passes on the nature of true belief in God in her very milk, she a mother who had a mother who had a mother who had a mother, each mother, by the sheer impulse of generations upon generations upon generations of motherhood in her, engenders the most powerful faith in a God impelling life. That is God: the impulse, the sacred impulse, of life, made sacred by generations upon generations upon generations of mothers.

She spilled wine on her bodice when she drank.

Cross-eyed, she looked at her glass quizzically, seeming not to understand why the glass was empty. Again, she held out her glass to me, which I refilled.

The mother, the great mother, is the source of faith in God, and she will sustain the faith, will sustain the basis of faith in life, in life eternal in this world, this world she herself gave birth to and nurtured and will never, ever allow to die. The mother of each and every one of us – each mother a mother from so far back in motherhood she is immortal – all become, all together, the great mother, and she is the greatest proof of a loving God.

Yet again, she drank down her wine and held out her glass to me for a refill, and I did.

Everyone was sure she was a spinster, a woman who never had a lover and who never gave birth, and, perhaps, repressed, but perhaps not, perhaps just sexless. We tried to be tolerant of her when she became drunk, which she did at these parties.

I accompanied her home, she stumbling and repeating over and over, Holy Mother of God, Holy Mother of God, Holy Mother of God.

Purification

He was a young tourist who wanted to go where no other tourists went, and on old, dusty buses he rode to remote villages in the stark mountains.

He had wanted to travel alone, and, alone, thought of himself as purifying himself. When he asked himself what he meant by this, he couldn't answer, not really, though it may only have been that he was confused and wanted to be clear about his life. Just twenty, he felt he must be clear about his life. But, in cheap hotel rooms, with a chipped enamel basin on a stand and an enamel jug of water in the corner of the room, he found he was not able to reduce his thinking and feeling to a simple essential, which would have been a purification. Some memory would come to him – a memory that had no reason to occur to him now, such as once when he tried to impress a group of people by speaking Greek but made a blatant error – and he would sense himself, yes, impure. Lying on his bed, hardly more than a pallet, he thought: just to be himself was to be impure.

This self, shivering, waited at dawn for a bus to take him to another village deeper into the mountains.

The village, made of small stone houses with roofs made of flat stones, seemed to be empty. Chained dogs barked at him as he walked through the lanes and up a dirt road leading to a mountain side. He stopped when he saw, behind a stone wall, people gathered in a cemetery. He heard wailing, high pitched wailing.

An old man from the group approached him, and he stepped back, but the old man made a gesture that he should come forward, by way of the open gate into the cemetery. He didn't understand what the old man said, but he smiled, and the old man took his arm to bring him into group of men and children, beyond them a ring of women in black, wailing. He saw, beyond the ring of wailing women, two men digging a grave. The wailing of the women rose higher and higher, with singing.

The men dug until one of them stopped, as if he had come to something that was no longer up to him to uncover, and the other man stopped also. They were replaced by a woman in black, a woman wearing a tight black cap and a kerchief tied tightly about the cap, who continued the digging with her hands, revealing fragments of wood and then a bone. She cleared the bone of earth.

Stupefied, the young foreigner stared as the woman uncovered bone after bone, which she placed on a large white cloth by the side of the grave. In the pit, the woman crossed herself and lifted out of the earth the black skull, and all the wailing singing stopped. Someone threw flowers into the pit. The grave-digger pulled away the last of the hair from the crown of the skull, wrapped it in a white kerchief, placed paper money on the wrapped skull and handed it to a woman, who cradling the wrapped skull, sobbed, and cried out as if for answers to her sobbing.

She placed more paper money on the skull and double-wrapped it in an embroidered cloth, then pressed the skull to her cheek. She kissed it, and when another woman came to take it away from her she held on to it, screaming, so the woman withdrew and the grieving woman sat on the ground and held the skull in her lap as the women in the pit continued to dig out bones, small bones, finger and toe bones, which were placed on the large cloth, a heap, and when all the bones, and, too, a gold tooth, were dug up from the mud, another woman washed them in wine and placed them in a small suit case, and women threw coins in among the bones.

When all the bones were exhumed, there was silence except for the wind. In the silence, the woman with the skull finally gave it up to a woman in black, who placed it in the suit case.

As a priest, in a cloud of incense, approached, the old man who had brought the foreigner into the group pulled at his arm to take him away.

He took him to a small cement building at a corner of the cemetery, and the old man opened the door and motioned for the young man to go in, which he, in trance of stupefaction, did. Inside was a ladder down to a space below, and the old man motioned the foreigner to go down, down into a windowless space filled with bones, piles of bones, skulls, pelvises, ribs, the long bones of countless arms and legs – and on the piles were bundles of bones, some of the cloths rotting, of the more recent dead. In a corner were stacks of suitcases and metal boxes, with names, and some with photographs.

When the young man turned to the old man, he saw he was smiling a wide smile.

Listen, listen: there is purification, there is.

Inspired by *The Death Rituals of Rural Greece,* Loring M. Danforth, Princeton University Press, 1982

The Vision

In his bedroom, dressing for work, he heard the cleaning woman come into the flat. He called out, as he always did, and she answered, as she always did, don't worry, but this morning her voice was low, which meant she was having trouble with her son.

He smelled clean laundry, and found her in the kitchen, standing at an ironing board and ironing one of his shirts. She was short, in a blue smock and slippers. She was a South American, from Uruguay, living now with her son in London for reasons that she never made clear. She didn't seem to have a husband. Her son was sixteen.

Though he knew only a little Spanish, asked her, Que pasa? This was the way they started out her one day a week job for him.

She shrugged. She said, todo pasa.

What's wrong? he asked.

Slamming the iron down on the shirt, she said, What's wrong? Everything is wrong.

I've got to get to work.

I know, I know. Is not important enough. You go to work.

Can you tell me in five minutes?

She propped the iron in the middle of his shirt, so he thought the cloth might be scorched. Her face was dark and smooth. There was Indian blood in her. I tell you like a sister, she said.

Yes, yes.

I tell you because I know you understand, like a brother.

What has happened to your son?

She raised her hands and clapped them over her head, then placed them on her head. I swear, she said, I swear that he no steal. Then she covered her face with her hands except for her tearful eyes.

Of course not, he said. Of course he wouldn't steal anything.

A wail came though her fingers. The police, the police come to our flat.

He put a hand on her shoulder. Don't get hysterical.

La policía, she wailed.

You are in another country now, and you don't have to get hysterical about the police.

He wasn't sure if the police in Uruguay were such that anyone there would get hysterical about a house visit by them. He was North American, and he knew very little about South America.

His daily wiped her eyes with the backs of her hands.

He waited.

She said, you know, he has his work in the chemist shop. Not good work, but work. The chemist say he, he take five pounds. It's me, it's me, who give those five pounds to my son. Me. He not take from the till.

And, of course, when the chemist accused your son, your son got angry.

Of course. Of course he get angry.

Of course.

My son no steal five pounds.

No.

He, my son, he throw the five pounds at the chemist and shout, 'take the five pounds my mother she give me. Take them.'

And what did the chemist do?

He call the police.

Your son shouldn't have got angry. You know and I know that the English do not like people to get angry. We're both foreigners here. We should try to behave like the English.

Yes, yes, I know. I tell him that. That is his mistake. But can he not get angry when the five pounds his mother give him the chemist say he take from the till? Who can not get angry with that?

Did the chemist check that the five pounds didn't come from the cash register?

Unfortunate it is, six pounds are missing from the cash. Not five. Six. If my son steal, he take six pounds, not five. No?

I see your logic.

My son, he no want to tell me, his mother, he lose his job, so all day he walk around London, come home at the same time he come home usually from his job. He no say anything. He no want his mother to know, to worry. Then, when we eat, the police come. Again, she put her hands over her mouth and wailed, faintly this time. They come to see if he at home, because he have to stay at home at night.

He looked at his watch. He would be late.

Will he have to go to court? he asked.

Court?

He is a British subject, isn't he?

Thanks God.

Has he spoken to a solicitor?

She leaned towards him to listen.

He should have a solicitor. He won't be deported, but he'll be tried.

Where from can he find a solicitor?

He felt she was taking his help too much for granted. She followed him into his small sitting room where, from a desk drawer, he took out the telephone directory A–D, and she watched him closely as he looked for the listing Citizens' Advice Bureau. This was an often repeated contradiction in him: he did and did not like to be imposed upon, and was both resentful towards his daily and curiously pleased with himself for allowing himself to be as he went down the list for a bureau close to where she and her son lived in Portobello. He wrote out the address on a piece of paper and gave it to her.

Tell him to go there and explain his situation.

She stared at the writing.

You understand?'

What you think, I'm stupid? Yes, I understand.

He remembered his shirt on the ironing board, the iron on it, but he didn't want to tell her to go back to it, as he felt the fate of her son was, rightly, more important than the fate of his shirt.

I must go to work, he said.

She didn't thank him. Staring at the paper in both hands close to his face, she went into the kitchen. He was not sure she could read.

When she came again the next week, she called him from the entry hall. He was in his underpants, and from behind the half-closed door of his bedroom he asked what she wanted. You come, she said. He put on his dressing gown and went out to where she, in her narrow, black coat and black, high heel boots, was standing next to her son.

Her son, who did not look Indian, must have had a British father.

He said, I want to thank you for your help.

I hardly did anything.

You did a lot.

What happened?

I was fined fifty pounds.

You pleaded guilty?

My solicitor from the Advice Bureau said it would be better to do that than plead innocent and to go to Crown Court, which would take a long time and be expensive. Then, for my mother, I wanted it to be over quick.

Innocent, his mother said, and he have to pay fifty pounds.

Her son said to her, you had to pay. I didn't have fifty pounds.

Her employer said to her, will you make coffee for the three of us?

She left to go to the kitchen.

Come into my bedroom with me while I dress, Charles said to the boy.

The boy sat on the edge of the unmade bed.

What will you do now?

I'll have to find another job.

Do you have any idea what?

No.

You can go on the dole.

Yes.

I'll give you fifty pounds.

The boy lay back on Charles' pillows without speaking.

I don't want to impose the money on you, of course. If you feel you can't take it, I'll understand.

He was aware of Fernando watching him put on

his trousers, his socks and shoes, and knot his tie in the mirror on the inside of the bedroom door.

The daily came in to ask where to serve coffee.

Again, he'd be late. In the sitting room, he said.

The furniture that came with the small, rented flat was frayed and old, but it was all velvet and shining dark wood. This flat in London, which was old but elegant, was, really, as foreign to him as it must have been to his daily and her son, who, like him, was being a little formal, both of them sitting upright in their armchairs and holding their cups and saucers.

Whenever the boy drank coffee he leaned his long, lean body over the coffee table so a mass of his curly black hair fell forward, picked up the cup, sipped from it, put it down, then, pushing his hair back from his forehead.

He said, you've got such nice place to live.

Thanks.

I hope my mother is a help to you.

I couldn't get by without her.

Leaning his head against the sofa cushion, for a moment the boy closed his eyes.

Where will you look for a job?

The boy opened his eyes and shrugged.

I suppose your friends can help you.

Most of my friends are out of work and on the dole.

Who are your friends?

Lazy lay-abouts, drop-outs.

They sound like good people.

They are. We all love one another and help one another, as much as we can help one another. A bunch came to my trial. You'd like them.

I'm sure I would.

Each one of us has a different nationality. Isn't that interesting?

It is.

The daily said to her employer, You be late for work.

Yes, yes.

But he didn't want to leave.

Tell me, if you could do anything in the world, what would you want most to do?

The boy turned his head sideways against the sofa cushion as though he were about to fall asleep. He said, I don't know.

His mother said, I, too, late for work, and she collected the coffee cups on a tray and brought them into the kitchen.

Business-like, he said to the boy, come with me back to my bedroom.

As though he were exposing everything there was to know about himself to the boy, he opened a top drawer of the chest of drawers and took out a stash of ten pound notes, folded and held together with a silver clip. Handing out five notes to the boy, he said, you don't have to tell your mother about this. A little thrill went through him.

What if she finds out I've got so much money?

Then tell her I gave it to you.

The boy counted the notes before putting them into his pocket. For some reason, his counting them, as if they were the payment of a debt owed to him, pleased the man.

He said, I'd like to know more about your friends.

We get on fine.

What do you do when you go out together?

We sort of roam around.

Roam where?

Here and there.

I had friends I could roam around with and get into a little trouble with when I was your age.

His daily came into the room. You really late, she said.

All right, he said. I'm going.

It took him fifteen minutes to walk to his office. As he walked, he thought about what he could do for the boy, who was intelligent and who spoke well. He wondered if he could at least introduce him to the children of his English friends. Trying to decide how this could be done – by inviting him and two or three of his friends' kids for, what? Tea? But not with himself as the only adult, and it'd be worse if he asked the kids' parents also, because what would they think of the boy's presence in his flat? He realized that he couldn't make the boy a part of the world he lived in now, not now.

After work, he had to go to a drinks party, then to a dinner party. He was tired when he got back to his flat. His suit smelled of cigarette smoke, and his body, too, smelled of smoke. Also, he was a little drunk, which he hated. He showered and put on pajamas and a dressing gown, and he sat on the sofa in his sitting room to drink orange juice. He didn't want to go to bed, but to be quiet, and, alone, withdraw from the world he lived in now. When he heard the door buzzer, it was as if he heard an echo of buzzers and telephones ringing and high voices and even strident laughter from the past day. The buzzer sounded again, and, frowning, he went into the entry where he picked up the answer phone and asked who it was.

This, too, sounded like an echo.

He pushed the button to release the catch on the street door. He opened the door to his flat, lit the light on the stairs, and waited for the boy, who smiled as he came up the stairs.

Isn't it late for you to be out?

What time is it?

Late. Does your mother know where you are?

My poor mother.

Come in

They sat across from one another with cups of tea and shortbread at the dining table. Between them were two silver candle sticks, which the boy's mother polished every week.

The boy said, I want to tell you I finally thought what I most want to do.

Oh?

I want to go to Uruguay.

To Uruguay?

None of my mother's family speak to her, so I don't have any relatives there. And I've never been.

You were born here?

My mother met my father there, but I was born here. My mother came looking for my father.

I see.

Now, I'd like to go – . He laughed. I was going to say 'back,' but I've never been, so I can't say I'd like to go 'back.'

Do you know what it's like there?

No. My mother doesn't talk about it. Do you know?

No, I don't.

Once, I met an Englishman, about your age, who told me a story about South America. I can't remember in what country it happens, and maybe still happens. The boys of the village go, once a year at a certain time, up into the mountains. They pull straws or something, and whoever pulls the shortest straw gets into a hole, and the other boys pile stones over the hole and leave just enough space for his to stick his arm out. Then they put a piece of horse meat on a stone just by the opening, and they go hide themselves behind rocks. They all wait, they wait sometimes for days, until an eagle comes down for the piece of meat. While the eagle is eating the meat, the boy under the stones reaches his arm out through the opening and grabs the legs of the eagle, and the other boys come out running and throw a net over the eagle. They take the eagle back to the village.

His voice went low, and the man leaned towards him to hear.

Then this ceremony takes place in the village square. The eagle is tied to the head of a donkey, and the eagle and the donkey are released into the square. On the roof tops and from windows, the villagers watch this really strange animal gallop and fly round and round, until it dies.

Until it dies.

The Englishman told me he saw it. Do you believe it?

I do.

I want to go see.

I think you should go.

A Mother and a Son

From the front window of our summer house, I saw my mother go down to the dock on the lake's edge and stand there for a long while, I thinking: Momma, jump and let go, for I could no longer bear her holding on.

I'll give her her name, Albina, an ancient Roman name.

I waited at the window, watched my mother, her back to me, standing on the dock, and I turned away.

Out of a door into the woods, I walked along a path that led to an abandoned apple orchard, and I leaned against the trunk of an apple tree and wept.

I was sixteen years old.

Returned to the house, I saw from the window that she was not on the dock. The sun was setting.

I went to her room. The door was shut.

In my room, on my bed, I heard from out on the dark lake the splash of oars hitting water and the clank of oars in the oarlocks. Whoever was rowing the boat was approaching the dock below the house, someone who would let the boat silently hit the old car tires used as bumpers alongside the dock, would secure the boat with a rope, would climb out and walk along the dock to the path up to the house, would come into the house, whose doors were never locked.

The rowing stopped, and with it the sounds of frogs and crickets seemed to stop too. The rowing started again, but at a distance.

Unable to sleep, I got up to find my mother. She was on the screened-in porch, on the glider, rocking back and forth slowly, her rosary gripped by both hands.

You can't sleep? I asked.

Oh, she answered, thoughts, just thoughts.

I sat with her and we rocked back and forth slowly together.

What thoughts?

I can't say. I can't.

No, she couldn't say.

Large-winged insects hit the screens about us.

She said, There is so much suffering in the world, so much.

We stopped rocking at the sound of the rowing of the boat out on the lake, below us in the dark, there where the dock was; the rowing stopped, and I thought that whoever was in the boat was looking up at us, sitting together in the lit porch, the person in the boat invisible in the dark; we listened, but the splashing of the rowing and the grinding of the oars in the oarlocks went on, passing us.

Always, throughout this story, I imagine someone at a distance from us looking at us, someone we can't see but who sees us.

I said to my mother, You love being here, I know you do.

Yes, I do, she said.

And we resumed rocking together, slowly.

That summer at the lake, where my family had a house, I remember as the time when I was most alone with my mother.

My father spent most of the week in the parish in the city, as to come to the lake house after his work would have been too far; also, I think he wanted to leave his wife to me, as if he had, long before, left her. He knew I could raise her spirits.

And for a while I raised her spirits, had her thinking about out immediate lives together rather than the world far outside us, there at the large clapboard and fieldstone house with views of the lake beyond pine trees, birch trees, oak trees.

Yes, I loved that place. And so did she.

Did I really feel that the suffering of the world was the cause of my mother's suffering? She didn't know the world, had only been as far as New York, years before, on her honeymoon with my father. Her disposition as a mother was to think of children, not of herself; was to think of the world, not herself, and for her the world was a world of suffering. Her selfless disposition would not allow her to indulge in thinking she herself suffered.

But now my mother and I were far from that suffering as a summer on a clear lake enclosed by reflected pine trees allowed us, the air redolent of resin in the hot afternoon, of the damp smell of mist that rose in the cool evening from the still lake, of the fresh smell of dawn through the open window.

The place was called a camp. Oh yes, I had a bright sensibility, and that sensibility was fulfilled by the bright summer. I could go on about the freedom of my sensitive five senses during that summer, a freedom I felt my mother was aware of, aware of her son growing into his sex, an awareness she took pleasure in. I would see her look, as if glancingly, at me lying in my bathing suit on a blanket in the sunshine, and I would catch that glance, which pleased me as much as I thought it pleased her. I went about all during the sunlit days in nothing but my tight, white bathing suit, barefoot, my exposed body tanned in its nakedness.

There were moments when I felt my mother, too, indulged in the freedom of her body, as when I persuaded her to take a bicycle ride with me along the country lanes, she who had never ridden a bicycle, but finally dared. She immediately found her balance, and in shorts and a loose blouse she laughed as she pedaled through the shadows of the trees, all her body in motion, delighted by the motion.

My mother could, yes, she could at moments – always, at moments, whatever it was she at the moment felt, for her feelings shifted constantly — be outwardly bright spirited. Then the shift, and she appeared, inwardly, to become dark. I want to believe she was in herself a woman who could and did enjoy a bright outward life, but whose inward life darkened all that was outside her. She would then close her eyes and frown, and so, too, would I close my eyes and frown. If she sighed, I sighed.

She joined me on the blanket in the sunshine, where I was trying in a desultory way to learn Latin. She wore a bathrobe, as it was still morning and she had woken not long before. I continued to try to memories Latin tenses and all the while I knew she was studying me.

And that apprehension came to me, as it so often did, that someone at a distance was aware of us, and watched us.

She lay sideways on the blanket beside me, a hand holding her bathrobe closed about her soft neck.

What are you reading?

I'm studying Latin.

Why Latin?

It's a basic.

You're always looking for some basic.

All of this was lightly said.

Pause, my mother shifting her body on a hip.

Well, she hoped I'd find the basic.

Thanks.

Another pause.

This was what she hoped for me: That I'd have a good, happy life.

And I hoped that her hope would come true.

It would.

I took great pleasure in these moments, especially as I knew that she could suddenly become strict by admonishing me for my being lax.

And I took special pleasure in the moments because they seemed to me always on the point of being let go of, as if they were held back from – what? – a helpless longing, in me as it was in my mother, but in her more helplessly.

And this was somehow in my love for my mother: that she would finally give in to her helplessness.

This is an insight that I leave as it is, because I had only a sense of it then, and if I were now to try to bring that deep, strange sense up to a level of understanding it, I would find myself indulging in what I must not allow myself to indulge in, whatever indulgence that may be. My self-indulgences, which are deep and strange, frighten me.

I had once told her that she was named after a martyr, who, born in the Roman city of Caesarea, in the 3rd Century AD, and at a tender age and a witness for Christ, was arrested as a victim of the persecutions imposed on Christians by Emperor Trajanus Decius of Rome. Saint Albina was listed in the Roman Martyrology. My mother smiled. She liked this historical reference to her name.

You're hot, she said, go cool off with a swim.

But I remained where I was, studying. To get my attention, she reached out to take the grammar book from my hand, and after she read a little she read out, Amo, amas, amat, amamus, amatis, amant.

I said, I love, you love, he/she loves, we love, you love, they love.

She laughed.

Saint Albina spoke Latin, didn't she?

She did.

She would have known those words.

She probably even spoke them.She let the book fall to the blanket and my mother said, Imagine.

I picked up the grammar book and, squinting, read: hic liber.

My mother touched my bare shoulder, then moved her hand round to hold my nape.

Your body is hot, she said. Go in for a swim to cool off.

She rose and I looked up at her. She looked down at me and said she would do anything for me to have a good, happy life.

And I said she made me feel that I was fated not to have a good, happy life.

Oh no, no, she didn't want me to feel that. How could she, a mother, wish anything for her son but that he should have a good, happy life? How could she, a mother, not do everything to save her son from what was bad, from unhappiness? She would sacrifice her life for my happiness.

Please, she must not say that, please.

From above, she continued to study me lying before her, and she said, Do you know how good looking you are?

I laughed. I didn't know, and had only my mother to tell me, and as my mother she would of could say this to me.

She allowed me my freedom. In the afternoon I crossed the lake in our row boat to visit friends.

The sun had just set across the lake when I returned to my mother, who was sitting on the glider on the screened-in porch.

I knew that she had not been waiting for me, as she would have wanted me to have a good time away from her.

In the kitchen I prepared some iced tea and brought out two glasses on a tray.

My mother had a pale face which appeared to be tucked in at delicate points, leaving her cheeks and under her chin and her neck smooth. She had blue eyes and black hair with streaks of grey in the natural wave above her bare forehead.

We drank our tea in silence.

My mother was frowning from her thoughts.

And I was thinking, too.

I said, the thought suddenly coming to me and surprising me: What has our religion given us to make us happy in this world?

Our religion? my mother said.

A soft warm breeze was soughing through the screens of the porch.

(Oh, give up with such soft, warm, soughing literary affectations, give up.)

I wondered why I had suddenly, surprisingly said that about religion, but at the same time I knew, because I was aware, as if it had become one with my wondering about everything, that the happiness my mother promised me she did not, herself, believe would come to me, not any more than she believed happiness would come to her. I knew, also, that I could not accuse her of being false, no, but I could accuse our religion, which my mother believed in as the very reason for living a life of suffering, which suffering promised another world in which we would be happy. And I knew that, as much as she insisted on that world, insisted on it to me, she did not believe in it, and I wanted her to admit her disbelief, or at least listen to my disbelief as a way of belying hers. It was as though my mother's will was her belief, her belief in her religion, and, finally, her belief in me, and, yes, I did want my mother to give up on her will, her willing her religion, her willing my happiness. I have no idea why I did want this. I did not believe in her, because, really, her will was too weak for her to sustain it in a convincing way, convincing to me and to her, however much she held on to it, however much she was frightened of letting go, however frightened I was of her letting go. I loved my mother.

She was agitated by what I had said, no longer rocking in slow rhythm with me, but herself impelling the rhythm in quick jerks with her feet on the floor, as if she were keening in quick jerks of her body. I became rigid, the soles of my bare feet rising to the heels, which scraped against the cement, then my soles falling flat, over and over.

My mother said to me:

You owe to our religion that you were born. God wanted me to stay in the world of our religion, so that you would be born.

And that should be enough for me to believe in our religion?

It should. She said, I did my duty according to our religion. You have our religion to thank for your life.

I didn't want to sit there, didn't want to listen; I didn't want to be her son, but wanted to get up, go out, along the dirt road out to the main road and – what? – hitch a ride to anywhere?

I stopped the jerking swing of the glider by slamming down my feet and I said, in a flash of spiteful anger:

I wish I wasn't born.

I saw the shock in her face, and I saw her hand rise

and for the first and only time in our lives together she hit me across my face, her face contorted. I sank back, motionless, and she too became motionless.

Then she almost shouted: I wished that I'd die. I wished it, but I didn't die, I lived, because it would have been an unforgiveable sin to want to die, and I lived to have you, to do my duty and have you and give you life with all the love a mother can have for a son. I lived for you.

And then I jumped up and did go out, along the dirt road in the dark out to the main road, where there were lights on posts that shone into the woods on either side, and when a lone car came along I drew back into the shadows of the woods not to be seen.

Do not think that I felt my mother's feelings towards me were incestuous, and that I was reacting against that. Incestuous feelings on her part would have been too obvious, and, obvious, banal; no, my mother's feelings towards me at this crisis – this sudden crisis – were deeper, for I wanted my mother to be a mother of great depth, deeper than sex. I had tried to inspire in my mother the spirit of her body, and, I suppose, of her sexuality, however vaguely, but not now. Now I was shocked by what I, at a deeper depth, wanted from my mother: wanted her to be a mother whose suffering I was born from, for I grieved so, grief that I could only sense was grief at suffering I was born with in her, as she perhaps was born of the suffering and grief of her mother, who was born of a grieving mother, born of a grieving mother, born of a grieving mother, back and back into the forests of North America, mother upon mother upon mother who, all together, were one great, suffering, grieving mother. Beyond generating life, this great mother grieved for life already generated in suffering. If she gave into her grief, if she did kill herself, she would have fulfilled my love for that great grieving mother, which love longed to be fulfilled in the ultimate cause to grieve, the death of a mother – a mother too great to be simply my mother, a great world-aware mother whose suffering was equal to her grief. She was powerful, that mother, in her grief, and in her grief she empowered in me a longing that shocked me, in the headlights of a passing car, for the power of the longing.

When I, trembling, returned to the house, I found the door to the porch open as I had left it. In the house, I called, Momma, from room to room, turning on lights as I went, and upstairs to her room, the door open and she not in it.

Now outside, I saw all the windows of the house cast light into the dark.

I went down to the dock, but she was not there; to our little swimming place where I sometimes found her sitting on a bench made of a plank on two rocks, but she was not there; even in the car parked under a pine tree, but she was not there.

I was trembling so my teeth did chatter.

I found her, featureless, standing among trees, and I had my vision of her: the vision of a great, dark mother.

My trembling gave way to shaking throughout me, terrified.

I called, softly, quizzically, Momma?

Silence.

Momma?

She said, Go to bed.

I took a step towards her.

Go, go, she said, go to bed.

And I took a step back.

The Wind

He made a date with a girl he met at a party to go to Symphony Hall, but she cancelled, and he went on his own. He was in the middle of a row, the seat next to him empty, the rest of the row filled. Just as the doors to the hall were being shut, the people along one side of him rose to let someone through to the seat next to him, a girl in a long black coat and a black beret, apologizing as she came in an accent that wasn't American. Standing at her seat, she took off her coat and then her beret, and her black hair, which had been tucked into her beret, fell loosely in damp tangles. She sat, folded her coat on her lap and leaned forward to stare at the empty stage. She was wearing a light grey polo neck pullover and a darker skirt. Slight, she was perspiring, maybe from having hurried, and strands of her hair were stuck to her pale cheeks.

The conductor came out and the girl leaned even further forward so he was able to see her better. When people around them opened their programmes to read the notes, the girl, he saw, realized she did not have a programme, which seemed so to disappoint her she fell back into her seat. He held out his open programme half way between them, and he was aware of her reading it in glances.

He noted that when they weren't playing, the trombonist and percussionist appeared not to be attentive to the music, but to be staring out into space.

At the intermission, he followed the girl out into the foyer, where he saw her try to buy a programme from an usher; but there were no more, and she stood in a corner. He walked back and forth over the carpet, the length of the foyer and back, and each time he walked towards her he drew back as if against being pulled towards her; finally, he gave into the pull, and as she watched him approach, her eyes within dark circles, he held out his programme to her.

Why don't you take this? he said.

She shook her head and delicately refused.

Please take it, he said.

She smiled – her smile, he thought, a little wan – and said, I should refuse at least three times before I accept.

She was staying in a service apartment near the hospital where she went for what she called treatments. She was, he found over the days he saw more and more of her, in the chronic phrase.

Her parents were dead, as were his. Her uncle came for their wedding, then husband and wife went to stay with the uncle. Walking in the public gardens, she told him that she suddenly felt very tired and that they should return to her uncle's apartment. With the heat of the summer, the uncle suggested that they go to the old ancestral house on the island.

Though they were traveling by day, she insisted on a cabin, and while she lay in her berth he looked about the ferry. He stood at the rail and watched the bleached islands, almost white, appear and disappear on the black sea.

A sense came over him that it was not his ill wife he was traveling with, but some other woman lying in the cabin. He went back to her. She was in the lower berth, and, in the dark cabin, he saw her hair falling from the small pillow. He undressed and leaned over her, and she, as if moving in her sleep, moved, leaving him enough space to lie down. He lay beside her and put his arm about her waist.

He noted that the swelling in her neck was red.

She became too weak, and they returned to stay with her uncle. She died on a day of intense heat.

When, after her burial on a day when the heat made all the heavy air waiver, he returned to the island.

On his way to his cabin, the slow rolling of the boat caused him to lurch from side to side, and just as he was opening the door into his cabin he lost his balance because of a roll and fell forward as the door swung open of itself. Sitting up in the top berth was a young woman combing her hair. Her comb held still, she frowned when she saw this unknown man, who, because of the continuing roll, was falling towards her. He tried to stop himself by grabbing hold of the handle to the toilet, but he pulled down on the handle and the door swung open and he fell further forward and stopped himself by taking hold of a rung of the metal ladder up to the top of the berth. The young woman pulled back from the light of the ceiling lamp into the shadow of her berth.

I'm sorry, he said. I'm very sorry.

The young woman didn't understand. She pulled a lock of her long hair over her mouth.

He smiled at her and left the cabin.

Walking along the deck, he was reluctant to go back to his cabin, because it was, he had checked, his cabin. As he opened the door, he saw the ceiling light was off but that the little reading lamp in the lower berth, his, was lit, and in that pale light he made out, on the upper level, the long hair of the young woman falling over the pillow and a little over the edge of the berth.

Moving quietly, he went into the toilet with his toiletry bag. Behind the closed door and in the harsh neon light, it occurred to him that she may have assumed his long absence meant he had found a place in another cabin, that she may have expected not him but a woman to sleep the night with her. But then, he thought as he undressed to his underpants, she would have known he'd be back because he had left his bag.

He lay his berth below her and shut off his reading lamp, and immediately, as if rising, he fell asleep.

In the morning, he untangled a leg from the narrow sheet and, lowering his head so as not to bump it against the berth above, he stood. The berth above was empty.

In the village, wind blew about him as he carried his bag through the streets just wide enough for a donkey. Wailing, bending in all directions, the wind rushed down side streets. But nothing else in the white village moved. The doors and shutters of the houses were closed.

With a large key he took from the side pocket of his summer jacket, he opened the door into the house. The big, marble-floored main room looked clean, but the wind, emitting a low groan, went in before him as if with a long neck and streaming hair and he followed the wind in.

He showered and shaved, then dressed in clean, loose clothes, and went out. On his way down a street, he passed a house that was being restored. It was reduced to grey cement outside, and inside workmen were plastering. The workmen's hair blew out and their shirts ballooned. Water thrown against a wall to wet it sprayed back at them. In the midst of the wind, the men worked silently. The wind pulled him down a narrow street then pushed him down another.

Nearing the beach, he saw the branches of the trees thrashed by wind, and when he reached the dunes the first person he met was a naked man with hair bleached russet by the sun, wearing a string of red beads about his neck, his oiled skin brown and his penis almost purple. He was buffeted by the wind. He appeared to him to belong to a tribe that had nothing to do with the island people, who had abandoned the island and left it to this tribe, which managed to survive the wind. On the beach, more naked people, men and women and children, huddled in small groups against the wind.

Sand rose up in long, gritty waves and, like the waves of the sea, rolled over and broke, and the naked people sitting in small groups on the beach turned their heads away.

Among swaying tamarisk trees was a cinder block coffee house. On a metal table outside the coffee house was a thrashing black plastic bag held down by a round beach stone. A young man and woman, naked, came out of the coffee house, and it was as though the wind brought from them a smell, that of rendered fat imbedded with hair.

At the end of the beach, in the dunes above the rocks, were the rusted remains of the chassis of a car, half sunk in the sand.

He took off his loose clothes and he stood naked among naked people, and in the scorching sunlight that familiar smell of his body rose up about him. He stepped away to step away from the smell, but it went with him as his body went with him, his body which filled him with so much disgust for the crooked hairs around his knobby nipples, for the moles and small polyps, for the pore-ridden skin, and, deeper, for the yellow fat, for the slimy muscles, for the bones, for the thick smell rising from his armpits, from his crotch, from his hairy asshole, from his burning flesh. He walked away from the beach, up to the rocks above, thinking he should not have come for this last visit to the island.

Naked, he strode along the path above the rocky headland and looked down and out to the sea, to where it turned from blue to green, and he saw a young woman swimming underwater. She rose to the surface to expel, air and to breathe in before she dived down again, her buttocks rising above the surface as she did. Underwater, she glided towards a flat rock on which seaweed swayed in the waves and then she rose up and stood on the rock.

She was the young woman from the boat.

Raising her arms so her tight breasts rose, too, she pressed her hands to her head as if to hold it against the long tresses of her hair blown out in tangles, and the wild wind raged about her.

Grief

Out in the yard, the dog was barking, and he went to a window of the sun room to look. Peg, a German shepherd, seemed to strain forward against being held back as she barked, with the resonating sound of mortar explosions, at the woods, where the late afternoon light among the autumn trees was dim. He pressed a hand against the window pane and his forehead against his hand to see into the woods, which began at the bottom of the lawn. The dimness was misty, the tall, thin trunks of oaks and pine and birch fading into the mist. There was nothing he could see in there that was causing Peg to bark so explosively and yet that kept her from rushing into the woods. Then he did see the high, grey ferns among the trees move, and a figure, just a little darker than the dimness, appeared. The figure was that of an old woman, carrying in either hand heavy jerry cans that made her stoop forward. Whoever the woman was, she stopped and stared at the house, and for a moment the dog stopped barking and became as still as the woman.

He was aware, all at once, of the cold glass beneath his hand, of the small expanding and contracting cloud his breath made, and, more, of the ruffles of the white curtains at his sides, and, even more, as if his vision had flattened out to the dimensions of the details of his immediate surroundings, of the wooden window frame and the sill.

Peg barked again, and he, startled into looking beyond the window, saw that the old woman had gone. Peg continued to bark, but diminishingly, and finally, with a growl, she came to lie on the deck below the window, just outside the door.

She had been the dog of his wife, and he imagined she believed her duty was to go on protecting the house for her, who was, Peg did not know, dead.

He turned away from the window to the sun room, which was as it had been when his wife died, with wood ash under the metal plate under the cast iron wood-burning stove, a crocheted throw blanket rumpled on a sofa, on the table before the sofa a newspaper folded open to an inside page in the midst of gardening and gourmet cooking magazines, one fallen to the floor.

He heard Peg bark again, but this time to let it be known that she was all pointed attention, and when he, once more at the window, saw Peg, her ears raised high, running to meet someone, he was sure, with a sense that nothing else could in any way be possible, that she would return with her mistress, her tongue lolling and bumping up against her mistress' thigh in her excitement to stay close to her. Peg didn't run around the corner of the house, though; without barking, she dashed into the woods, jumping high over the ferns, and she emerged with a neighbour, whose house was in the next clearing in the woods along the path. She was carrying a brown pot by its two jug handles.

He opened the door onto the deck and went out to meet her.

Her breath steamed about her head, and her greying hair appeared to be lightly frosted. Holding out the pot, she said, I brought you a meal.

Taking the pot from her, he quietly said, Thanks, but, again, his awareness became fixed on the details nearest him: the heavy brown pot and the two handles and the congealed juice around the rim of the lid.

I know you like baked beans, she said.

He tried to force himself to concentrate on her, her high cheekbones, her sharp chin, the fine wrinkles at the corners of her eyes and lips. She blinked a lot, and the corners of her mouth twitched. She wore no makeup.

Come on in, he said.

You're sure you want me?

Come on. Even if I didn't want you, I know it'd be good to have someone in the house with me.

She frowned a little. He always spoke to her in a way that could be offensive, but he didn't know why he did this; nor, he thought, did she know why. She accepted the offense with that little frown, then, evidently sure that it wasn't meant, she smiled. He made himself smile. But I really do want you to come in, he said.

Peg followed them inside, where she lay flat near the door, her long, narrow chin stretched out on the floor, her eyes open. She sighed.

He switched on the lights in the sun room.

If you don't mind my being bossy, his neighbour said, I'd suggest putting the pot in the oven to heat the beans.

He asked, Have you eaten?

She made a gesture that could have indicated yes or no, as if to say either would have been to assume too much.

Tell me.

Not really.

Then eat with me.

I don't want you think I brought the beans expecting to stay and eat them with you.

I'd never assume any expectation from you as great as that.

Without saying yes or no, she went with him into the kitchen where he placed the pot of beans on a rack in the oven.

What about your husband? Wouldn't he like to join us?

Oh no.

Why not?

I told them that you'd want to be alone, that I'd bring you the pot of beans and leave.

And here you are, staying.

He shook his head. While waiting for the beans to

heat up, he asked, how about some wine?

Wine?

After opening a bottle on a counter, he took two delicate, long-stemmed glasses from a cupboard above, and, the bottle in one hand and the glasses held by their crossed stems in the other, he told her to go before him into the sunroom, where the overhead lights blazed. The windows were now black, dripping with condensation.

She sat in an armchair, he in the middle of the sofa. As he poured out the wine, he saw, on the page the newspaper was turned to, a photograph of an old woman in a devastated main street of a town, her back to him, carrying two large plastic jerry cans along torn up trolley tracks. There was no one else anywhere in the photograph.

When does the cleaning woman come? his neighbour asked.

He handed her a glass of wine across the table. She comes tomorrow.

I just wondered, if you'd like me to put a little in order, but only if you want.

No, I don't want.

I'd just like you to know that I'm always there if you'd like help of any kind.

He said, from the back of his throat, Oh, I'd like help, and, as if the only creature that could give him help were the dog, he called, Peg. She rose, and, her body swinging, didn't come to him but walked around the room, then, in the middle, stood motionless and appeared to wait. Peg, come here, he called again, but the dog did not respond to him. She sat, lowered herself to the floor, her head held up, waiting.

She's waiting for her mistress, he said.

And I pray she will come back for her.

Suddenly moved by these words, he, unable to speak, raised a hand high, then let it fall on his head. As though he caught himself in a posture that he would have, in any one else, considered posturing, he dropped his hand and reached for his glass and said, hoarsely, but she won't.

When our son died, I believed, not by conviction but instinct, that he would suddenly appear, not miraculously, but matter-of-factly. I couldn't understand why he didn't. There seemed to me no reason, no reason at all, why he shouldn't.

How long did that last?

He died – when? – twenty years ago, and I still see no reason why he shouldn't open the door one day and come into the house.

I have to say I hope I won't go on believing she'll come back. I hope I won't go on believing it, because I know she won't, and I'm not someone to believe in something that doesn't happen.

No doubt it's a weakness in me, but it's not anything I can help.

I've never considered myself, and will never consider myself, a helpless person.

I think I am.

He stood and went to Peg, and he pulled at the hair at the back of her neck and shook her head, saying, She isn't going to come back, Peg, to which Peg looked up at him, her lower lids heavy. She can't come back, he said, and Peg stood and slowly lumbered out of the room into the darkness of another room.

As he paced back and forth, tears ran down the sides of his nose and, round his lips, to his chin.

I'm sorry, his friend said.

He said, Not only do I insist on not believing that she can come back — when I knew she was dying and nothing could be done to keep her alive, the thought — no, something deeper than thoughts, and maybe deeper than any feeling — came to me that I wanted her to die because life was so unbearable to her. He pulled at his thick, grey hair, and, his voice rising in pitch, he said, I wanted her to die, and on the last word his voice broke.

Her mouth opened, but it was a long moment before she asked, the word hardly more audible than a breath, Why?

His jaw dripping tears, his voice still high and on the edge of breaking, he said, at the depth of that instinct that is supposed to be in everyone, why didn't I want her to live? Why, at that depth, did I want her to die? You want to know why?

She winced.

He opened his hands wide and held them, palms

out, at his sides. I wanted her to die to the horrors of the world we have to live in day after day after day.

She lowered her head, and when she raised it, she said, I don't understand.

I didn't think you would.

She waited a moment, considering whether or not she should stay. She said, The beans should be warm. She would stay, because, he saw, she had made up her mind that, however offensive he was, he needed her.

She helped him set two places on the dining room table, and she brought in the pot and served the beans from it. And she tried to keep up conversation about the neighbours, about how John and Catherine were going to Europe for the holidays, how Paul and Sharon, instead of traveling this year, were going to stay around and were hoping for a lot of snow over the winter because they'd bought expensive skis and all the gear that went with skiing, how Margaretta, months after the death of Jim, was beginning to date, and everyone thought that good for her.

Good for her, good for them, he said.

Yes, good for them, she insisted. He's a widower, has three grown children Margaretta is looking forward to meeting, and has asked her if she'd like to go to some Caribbean island to learn fly-fishing.

Sitting back in his chair, he said with a little snort, Why can't you be more straight about what you're trying to tell me?

You know very well what I'm telling you.

Tell me.

She put her fork down on her plate and placed her hands on either side of the setting and, leaning over the table towards him, she said, with an edge of accusation, tell me what reason you have for thinking the world is horrible.

For a second I thought you'd be more original than that. For a second I thought you might say something I hadn't heard before. For just a second. I'll bet you're now going to tell me that compared with almost the entire rest of the world, I've got it good, I've got it more than good, I've got it great, and have no reason at all for thinking the world is horrible.

You do have it great.

I do, I do. I have it so great that I live in a big, colonial style house, with antiques, a wine cellar, and an alarm system connected directly to the police station so I can sleep in peace because I'm safe.

Don't forget you worked hard for it all.

I worked very hard, with an office overlooking the Public Garden and bonuses of half a million a year and first class travel around the world and stays in the most luxurious of hotels.

Should you have denied yourself all that?

Not for anything, no.

If anyone is going to have it all, why shouldn't you? The fact is, you weren't born in some devastated ex-

Soviet country, you don't have to worry how you're going to eat and keep warm, you don't have to be anxious about what will happen to you if you become sick or an old age pensioner. The world is not horrible for you.

I didn't say it is for me.

And don't tell me that you feel the way you do about the world because most of it is horrible. Don't tell me, because, as horrible as you know it is, you don't do one thing – not one Goddamned thing – about it.

A terrible tiredness came over him, and with the tiredness a sense of the insupportable weight of his body. His head seemed to wobble. He said, no, not one thing, not one.

Don't be a hypocrite about the world.

He looked away, at the tall antique dresser on the other side of the room with rows of plates standing on the shelves, the plates decorated with old time bucolic scenes of spring planting, of summer fruitfulness, of autumn harvesting, of sleigh rides in the winter snow.

He said, I do feel very tired.

Of course you do.

And yet I think it'd be selfish to go to bed so early. There's so much that needs to be done.

Allow yourself the selfishness. She got up and picked up the dirty plates from the table.

He got up also. Leave all this for the cleaning lady tomorrow.

She placed the plates back on the table.

Did I have a coat? she asked.

You didn't.

No, I didn't.

She seemed not to know which way to leave the house, but, as if her disorientation itself brought her to him, she said, I'm sorry.

I know you are.

I mean, I'm sorry for what I said, which may have sounded offensive, but, really, I meant it to help.

I'm sure you did.

Look, grief always brings with it the feeling that the world is horrible, so that you find yourself looking for reasons in the world for its being as horrible as you feel it is. I know, I've been there.

And you got over the feeling?

I got over it by repeating to myself, over and over, how lucky I am. She put her hands on his shoulders. Keep telling yourself how lucky you are.

I'll do my best.

She dropped her hands, but instead of leaving, she stood in front of him, searching his eyes. He closed his eyes, and when he opened them he saw that she was opening the door to go out, and she didn't look back before she shut the door behind her.

He called Peg, but she didn't come, and he went through the rooms looking for her, lighting lights as he went. He found her lying by the door that led downstairs to the garage. She stood and faced the door, which meant she wanted to go down; why she did, he had no idea, but he opened the door for her and she quickly slid past the edge. As intent as she was to go down into the garage, she must have had a reason. He left the door ajar, and, shutting off the lights as he retraced his steps, he went into the bedroom, the master bedroom, which was where his wife, alone, had spent her last week. He lay on the bed and shut off the bedside lamp.

In the dark an old woman appeared, carrying two large plastic jerry cans of water.

Tell me what you know, he said to her.

She put the jerry cans down. Tell you? You want to hear?

I want to hear.

You want to hear about the rape of women and men, too? You want to hear about men, women and children tied together and blown up, their remains thrown into a ditch for dogs to unearth? You want to hear about the bloody handprints of torturers on a wall? I can tell you.

Tell me, he said.

About gardens that are dug up where the mutilated bodies of the dead were buried, missing eyes, ears, limbs, genitals? About mass graves?

Tell me, he said, smearing tears across his face, tell me more.

The Silver Conch Shell

He wandered about the room, touching, as if his merely touching them would put order among them, spectacles, an alabaster bowl, a small bronze statue of a girl, a hair brush, a silver conch shell.

She was about to ask him, didn't he have his college studies to do? but he appeared lost to everything but touching the disordered objects in the room.

He picked up the silver conch shell and examining it he asked, Where is this from?

I don't recall.

Here it's been from before I was born, and I never quite noticed it before now.

From some trip your father and I took.

The silver conch shell held tightly, he walked about the sitting room and stopped and turned to her and asked, What should I do?

You expect me to tell you?

I expect you to tell me that at my age it's all fantasy.

Making a dismissive gesture, she said, It is fantasy.

He turned away.

What was not fantasy, she thought, was his helplessness, his hopelessness, was the deep need in him to submit to what made him helpless and hopeless.

And she felt she must submit to his youthful help-lessness, even hopelessness, for his sake, and she heard herself say, You should ring him.

In his distraction, he said, Oh, what I should do.

Ring him.

He won't speak to me.

Almost aggressively, she insisted, Then you will know for good that he won't, and get over him. Go, ring him.

This was everything he needed to hurry past her to go into the study, and passing he held out the silver shell to her; she took it, and as she studied the shell wondering if the spiral revolved in silver all through to the centre, she heard him say, That's it, then, and he paused and said, Good bye, and there was silence.

She was about to go into the study to see how he was, but, startled by the ringing of the telephone, she became still and listened to him say, Thank you, thank you so much for ringing back, thank you, thank you, yes, yes, thank you so much, and she sat back and closed her eyes.

Oh, my son, she thought, oh, my son.

Our Lady of the Beautiful Window

The spires of the cathedral rose from the flat, pale green fields of spring wheat. There was heavy traffic in what was no longer the town he'd known, but a city. The buildings were new and had wide, stark windows.

Park here, she said.

He didn't like to be told. Where? he shouted.

There, there.

He quickly parked the car in a space by a kerb, limited to only one hour.

Here you are, she said, no doubt waiting for me to go look for a hotel with a garage.

Angry, he waited in the car and watched her cross the traffic-dense street as if she knew where she was going, and it seemed minutes later that she came back and said, I've found one, and I've got a map to show us how to get through the one way streets. The setting sun was flashing off car windows, so he could hardly see the street signs and red and green lights, but she directed him to a modern hotel with a yard behind where he parked the car. Their room looked out over the darkening yard.

She said, We'd better get to the cathedral before it closes.

With her map, she led the way to the old town. The only person they encountered was an old man in a blue smock who stood against a stone wall and who looked away as they passed.

She went on ahead, hurrying along a cobbled street and she turned a corner. Through an arched gate way in an old stone wall, he saw standing before the porch of the cathedral. When he approached her, she said, It's closed.

She found a restaurant in the new town.

While they were eating, he said, I remember an old restaurant in the old town.

You do, do you?

It was run by an old woman. I remember the floor was flagged with stone, and the restaurant smelled like a stone cellar. I remember the old woman, without being asked, bringing glasses and a carafe of wine, then soup bowls, those heavy, deep, white soup bowls, and a metal tureen of potage which she carried by its handles with a dish towel and placed on the table, where it steamed in the chilly air. We served ourselves. The big ladle was dented. That was ten years ago,

In the morning, he got up before her and sat in a chair before the window that looked out onto the back yard, where a young man was holding the front wheel of a bicycle off the ground and rotating it, so its small, rapid clicks became a whir. A woman came into the yard pushing a bicycle. By the time his wife got up there were ten people with bicycles in the back yard; they spun their wheels and talked quietly.

He said he'd go now to the cathedral, but she said she'd want breakfast first. He insisted, he wanted to go now. She said, Go, go, and gave him the map as he wouldn't be able to find his way on his own.

He didn't take the map, but walked the narrow cobbled streets, wondering how he would leave her, his feelings so suddenly violent that he wondered if the only resolution was for him to kill her, yes, kill her, throttle her to show her what he felt. She reduced every expression of feeling he had to an accusation that he had no feelings, none for her, not for anyone, not at all, and this enraged him so he shouted, you think I have no feelings, you think I have no feelings? and she stood closer to him to stare into his eyes and dare him to let her know the feeling he had. Perhaps she was right, perhaps he had no feelings.

After a few wrong turns he came to the cathedral. In the inside dimness shone a distant blue light among the high pillars, and it was for this that he had come, to see again the lady of the beautiful window.

About the Author

An American who became British and who now resides permanently in Italy, David Plante's work includes novels such as *The Ghost of Henry James*, *Slides* and *The Darkness of the Body*. He also received critical acclaim for *Difficult Women*, a memoir of his relationships with Jean Rhys, Sonia Orwell, and Germaine Greer. The Francœur Trilogy – *The Family*, *The Country* and *The Woods* – was widely praised. He has been published in the *New Yorker* and *Paris Review*. A fellow of the Royal Society of Literature, he has received many honours, including a Guggenheim Fellowship and an American Academy and Institute of Arts and Letters Award.

OTHER BOOKS BY GREY SUIT EDITIONS

Donald Gardner
New and Selected Poems 1966–2020
£14.95

Anthony Howell
The Step is the Foot
Dance and its relationship to poetry
£14.99

Gwendolyn Leick
Gertrude Mabel May
An ABC of Gertrude Stein's Love Triangle
£14.99

Gwendolyn Leick
Franckstrasse 31
£10.95

Walter Owen
The Cross of Carl
AN ALLEGORY
Preface by General Sir Ian Hamilton
£9.95

Iliassa Sequin
Collected Complete Poems
£14.95

We also publish chapbooks by Donald Gardner, Alan Jenkins,
Fawzi Karim, Lorraine Mariner, Kerry-Lee Powell, Pamela
Stewart, Rosanne Wasserman and Hugo Williams